Sin on a Vengeful Heart

SINS
BOOK FOUR

RHIANNON FUTCH

Contents

One

JASMINE

I am still watching the door when Father Neally runs in his key in hand, hell bent for the door I am standing in front of. Stepping to the side I watch as he jams his key into the hole and starts chanting as he forces it to turn. I pull power to me as he painstakingly turns that key. Leonidas has come to stand on my left, a long sledge hammer over his shoulder. Scarlett is to the right of me, a hand on my shoulder as we watch. The lock clicks and we brace ourselves for what is to come.

To say we were not prepared for the flood of melon-size spiders that spread like a horrible black wave from the open doorway is an understatement.

The power I pulled before the door opened nearly flees from me in my horror at seeing those things spreading out. I grab it and hold on, sending sprays of energy to zap the fuzzy bastards. Scarlet and Leonidas are kicking, stomping and punching their way through, Leonidas's sledge left forgotten on the floor somewhere under all this. Then Father Neally roars, his form rippling into that of a huge bear. He stomps spiders and smashes them against the wall with his body as he pushes his way into the library. It is disgusting. Spider guts are embedded in his fur. That's going to be fuck all to get out.

We get just enough of the spiders in the house killed to start following Father Neally into the library. It is dark as a tomb so I send light balls flying through to give us just enough light to see the spiders. As I get into the library a spell that Hekate taught me flashes in my mind and I kneel to touch the floor, punching a spider that runs at me as I go. Yeesh. I don't mind spiders mostly, but this is creeping me the fuck out. The slime of spider guts on my hand is the most disgusting feeling. Hands on the floor I recite the spell in a whisper, sending a spider killing pulse of energy through the building. I hear Leonidas and Scarlett grunt in pain, while something bigger sounding screams. Without the noise of killing these big ass spiders we hear Father Neally fighting something. Running into the more open part of the library we slide to a stop when we catch sight of Father Neally fighting a spider that makes his bear form look small.

"Holy shit."

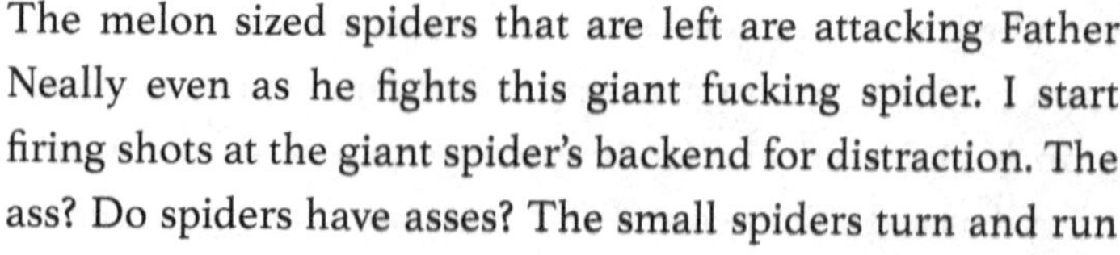

The melon sized spiders that are left are attacking Father Neally even as he fights this giant fucking spider. I start firing shots at the giant spider's backend for distraction. The ass? Do spiders have asses? The small spiders turn and run at me, Leonidas and Scarlett jump in front of me, kicking those things for the cheap seats. Scarlett gets a particularly good kick in and I yell, "Score!"

She jumps, "What the hell Jasmine?"

Leonidas laughs as I answer, "That was a great shot, it definitely deserved a cheer."

I hit the giant spider with a shot of fire and it freaks the fuck out, spinning around and screaming. Father Neally takes the distraction to slam his body against a shelf, killing the small spiders still attacking him. The fire on the giant spider goes out and she rushes at Father Neally. He meets her with a leap, crashing into her head as I shoot her from behind. The giant spider starts trying to back away from Father Neally and my shots.

I feel a tickle on my leg and I kick out, one of those damn melon size spiders goes flying. "We are getting an exterminator by the house ASAP, I never want to see another fucking spider in the house again."

Leonidas throws a spider at the wall, "Aw, I wanted to keep one. They are kind of cute."

"Do not fucking play about that shit Leonidas," Scarlet huffs as she kicks another spider like she is going for gold, "I see you with a spider and I am burning the house down with you in it."

The giant spider is facing toward me right now and I take the shot, hitting one of her huge eyes, it pops with a disgusting sound, goo flying in a spray. Father Neally darts forward and brings a paw down hard on the spiders head. It falls unconscious to the floor and Father Neally stands on his back legs, putting his front paws together he swings and hits the spiders head with all he's got. The head detaches from the body, flying a few feet before hitting a wall and falling to the floor, it rolls a bit, goo oozing from it.

Father Neally flops down to sit, slumped forward a bit and panting.

Before I find my own spot to rest I ask, "Father Neally, you good?" He nods with a bear snort and doesn't move much more than that.

Two

Sitting down next to Father Neally I ask, "What the hell happened here? Do giant fucking spiders invade on the regular?"

His form ripples and the somewhat portly human side of Father Neally is sitting next to me, "There has never been an intrusion into the library like this. Insects have a difficult time getting here because it is outside of time. The protections surrounding this place make it very difficult to find, and breaking into it is even more challenging."

Frowning I say, "I have to ask, how did this happen if that's the case?"

"I know as much as you right now. When you," a spider runs at him and he bats it at the wall with a wave of his hand, "called was the first I knew of it. That spider was brought here intentionally to keep us out. Since I didn't get a warning from the wards—"

"Why would you get a warning from the wards?" I watch him flinch when I ask, "are you a guardian too?"

"Erm," he scratches at his neck looking away, "something like that. It isn't important right now. What is important is who did this and why. We are going to need to go through the library and figure out what is missing. Luckily, there is a very old spell on the library that makes any space left empty glow. Only the spaces that have books assigned, or items. We should call Nia and Caden, they are the ones that tend the books."

"I'll send them each a message to meet us here. Let's see how they arrive."

A slow smiles spread across Father Neally's face, "You are much more devious than I gave you credit for. I like it. Send the messages."

⌁

We watch as Nia and Caden arrive after first bashing at their doors, Caden dashes in, his face scrunched up as he shouts, "What did you do?" He skids to a stop when Leonidas steps between us, a growl in his throat that gives me the shivers and violence in his stance. Nia carefully picks her way through, analyzing everything while Caden yells, "I knew you were a poor replacement! It should have been one of us! What did you do to our beautiful library?" Caden moves to go around the angry vampire before him and Leonidas' arm shoots out to hook Caden's waist and toss him across the room. Caden lands with a hiss, "Mind your business pretty boy! This is between me and the bitch!"

Leonidas rolls his shoulders, "She is my business. Call her bitch again and you'll be my business."

Caden crouches and Leonidas changes his stance slightly, bracing himself for impact. Father Neally steps between the two of them, "Knock it off or I will knock your heads together."

Nia takes the opportunity of momentary silence to call me over to the spider's body. "Smell it, the magic of the one that created this left the scent of that magic user. If you ever smell it again, you will know who has brought this spider here."

Leaning over the spider I sniff, lightly, in expectation of a foul smell because dead spider. What I am greeted with instead is the scent of burnt oranges and stale coffee. It surprises me and I look over at Nia, "What did you smell?"

She says, "You first."

"Burnt oranges and stale coffee? Does all magic leave a smell this odd?"

She shakes her head, "No, the scent is unique to the user. And yes, because the scent is unique to the user. Your magic smells much like you; wild roses, earth, and rain. Mine smells of mint and camellia."

Father Neally leans over the spider and inhales deeply, "Do any of you recognize this scent?"

Something tickles at the back of my mind, like I should remember it. "I feel like I recognize it from somewhere but I don't know where."

Nia nods, "You will recognize it when you scent it next. Now, the library is disgusting. Do you want to know how to clean it with your magic?"

"Yes, please!" She nods and begins the spell as I watch. Her magic is so fine and delicate, I understand why it would smell of mint and camellia. I won't be able to do the spell quite the way she is, I am not so delicate with my workings.

Perhaps a result of my training with Hekate who is always much more concerned with the results than how I got there. I kind of love that about training with her, when we get to train in the real world. She has been incredibly busy of late. Nia finishes the spell and her magic pulses through the library. Just that quick the mess and the bodies are gone. A thought occurs to me, "Nia, where did all the mess go?"

She blushes, "Maybe don't worry about that this one time. However, you should have a place in mind when you clean an area. The local dump is generally a good place."

Chuckling quietly, "I hope I am never your enemy." Her blush grows and I turn my attention to the others to give her some time to compose herself. Leonidas and Scarlett are standing near each other glaring at Caden while he speaks to Father Neally in a language I don't recognize. My eyes flick back over to my lovers, if I had to guess, they understand what Caden is saying. Dammit. Now I have to add learning as many languages as I can to my ever-growing to-do list. Fucking bullshit. I glance back at Nia, "Do you know what language Caden is using?"

She focuses on him and says, "Hmm, Elvish. You aren't missing anything. None of what he is saying is very complimentary of you."

"Super. That is the one I will learn first then. Jackass."

Nia's eyes widen, "Who are you going to get to teach you?"

"I haven't gotten that far, why?"

She sighs in what looks like relief, "Look, just stay away from most Elves. It is really difficult to tell which ones will be honest and which would like you as a pet. Here, I will gift you the language. I don't want you finding trouble because Caden has no manners." She reaches up as she whispers something I don't understand and touches the third eye area of my forehead. I feel a very strange sensation of something crawling into my head, then it settles and I tune in to what Caden is saying. I understand it. All of it. Fuck yeah! I start to pay attention to what he is saying as he disparages my parents for their shitty genetics and suddenly Leonidas and Father Neally are pulling me off of a very bloody Caden.

I can hear Scarlett and Nia laughing behind me. Leonidas puts a hand to the side of my face and gently pushes me to look at him, "Are you back with us?"

"I think so? Did I attack Caden?"

His lips twist in a wry smile, "What is the last thing you remember?"

"Well, I remember that," I don't know if Nia wants everyone to know she gave me the knowledge of the language so I decide to keep that to myself for now, "I was listening to Caden and suddenly understood what he was saying just as he started," turning my head to look at him I grit out, "trash talking my dead parents."

Caden's eyes widen as Leonidas gently turns me back towards him, "And he found out what fucking around like that brings. Are you in control now? You able to keep from killing your coworker if we let you go?"

"I think so. Assuming he can keep his filthy mouth from talking shit."

A rumbling chuckle vibrates Father Neally's chest, "I think Caden can manage to do that. Or we can just let you kill him. His choice."

Caden gasps as I smile, "I can live with that."

They release their hold on my arms and Leonidas tugs me into his. He whispers into my ear, "You are going to have to offer a more believable explanation later."

I nod my head in the pretense of snuggling closer as Father Neally says, "Now that's settled, we need to figure out what is missing."

Nia and Caden head for a set of shelves and we all follow. We pass through four aisles before they stop as one looking at a faintly glowing spot where a book should be. Caden swallows and Nia pales. They start moving again, faster this time. They stop at two more spaces and the second one has Nia so pale I am concerned she will pass out. Caden's face is so pinched I could almost forget what he said about my parents.

Three

Nia and Caden lead the way back to the central area of the library, where there are tables and chairs. We all have a seat and wait for them to speak. Nia sits with a thump as though her legs were giving out. Caden isn't doing much better though he sits without thumping the seat.

Nia looks up from the table, "It's bad. I don't know if they knew what they were after or if they had enough time to browse but..." she sucks in air as if starved, "they managed the three worst possible books to be out in the world."

Caden speaks, his voice just over a whisper, "Hekate's Gift. The Book of Life. Persephone's Escape."

Father Neally gasps, "We have to get those back!"

"Not that I disagree, but I don't know why this is so terrible? I recognize Hekate and Persephone. Knowing what Hekate has taught me, I can kind of see why her writings maybe shouldn't wander out in the world. She seems to favor some... dangerous things to put it mildly. But Perse-phone, wasn't she like a spring maiden?"

Father Neally snorts, "Before she got out of her mother's clutches yes, spring maiden was exactly what she was forced to be. Once she escaped to be with Hades, she became. And what she became was Queen of the Underworld. It was as Queen of the Underworld that she wrote Persephone's Escape. The things in there are not things for humans, or even most witches, to be reading ever. Most of us don't have the willpower for it. The Book of Life, the things they say in the movies about it brush up against the truth. In the most abstract of ways. Then Hekate's Gift. Gift is an interesting term, I often wonder if it was meant to be tongue in cheek. A lot of what is in there are creative ways to make things happen or stop."

He shakes his head, "We must get those books back. At any cost. The world depends on it.We have another issue to handle as well. Because while those three are the ones we least want wandering the planet, we have others here that need to stay here. I don't know if any of you have noticed, but Frank and Lacey never showed up. The door alarms here should have all gone off and did not. Our security system seems to effectively be offline. With the absence of those two it could mean one of two things. They are in deep trouble or they will be in deep trouble."

"Shit. Ok. I definitely understand now. We are currently fucked and will become progressively more fucked if we cannot manage to get those books back. While we are at that we need to figure out Frank and Lacey. Super."

Four

Leaving the library back into my house, we all head for Frank's house with a pause for me to change my clothes. Walking through the library door into his place seemed like maybe not a great plan, in case of traps or, pissing off an already cranky wolf that definitely did not seem to like me at all.

Being bitten by an angry wolf does not sound like my idea of a good time in any way. Stepping into my bedroom and shutting the door, I shed spider - ick covered clothing and walk to my closet while using the cleaning spell on myself. It stings, but that's fine. At least the spider ick is gone. I grab fresh clothing, jeans and a band tee. Bon-Jovi still makes me weak at the knees. I start to grab a pair of shoes only to find that they are a mess once again and some of them are missing. "UGH! Listen here you thieving little fuck! I will snatch you out of the wall and turn you into a lawn ornament! Dogs. Will. Pee. On. You. Put my shoes back and stop stealing them or face life as a flamingo on my lawn with a particular allure to dogs looking for a spot to pee!" Going through the shoes I quickly find a match and stuff my feet into them as I head for the door. "Fucking asshole creature."

Everyone is watching as I exit my bedroom, I scowl at them and they smile while moving toward the front door.

Most of us being vampires we just walk there, it isn't far and we are pretty fast. With it being very late, we have less worries about being seen. The Father Neally is faster than I would have expected and Nia just uses her magic to keep up. Before long we stand in front of the wolf's house. It is dark and looks as abandoned as it feels. Before anyone opens the door, Nia checks for traps. Finding none, she uses magic to unlock the door. We walk in and the dust is thick everywhere. No one has been here in a very long time. We can't even smell the wolf but for faint and old scents left behind in spots he spent more time in. He is very neat, things are not left laying around, no food left out to spoil. It would appear, on the surface at least, that wherever he is, he chose to go there.

Leaving the way we came we stop on the sidewalk, turning back to look at the house. Father Neally says, "It didn't look like he was forced to go anywhere."

Leonidas shakes his head once, "No, it doesn't look that way."

Caden sticks his chin out, "Magic could have set his house to rights after a brawl, no matter what the place looked like. We can't make and accurate judgement based off what his house looks like."

Father Neally looks relieved, "You're right. He could have been forced out. Thank you Caden, for reminding me."

Caden ducks his head, I don't think he expected praise for that. He mumbles, "Thanks. We should go check Lacey's place."

Lacey's place isn't far and it looks much the same. Empty and abandoned. Nia checks things again and lets us inside. I breath deeply but I can't smell any magic here. Nia looks sharply at me and I know she isn't finding any magic in the air either. "Shouldn't this place reek of magic?" I ask and she nods. Father Neally looks grim as we step lightly through the rest of the house. Stopping before an odd stretch of wall in the hall Father Neally touches a hand to it and a door reveals itself.

He opens it and we all follow him in. It is obviously a room set aside for magic based on the altar and occult books everywhere. I can smell her magic in here, just the faintest scent of it, it smells awful. Strawberry scented marker and glass cleaner. Yuck. Another area of the room smells of the same magic as the spider did, burnt oranges and stale coffee. I look to Nia and she walks over, as she inhales her eyes widen and her nostrils flare. Father Neally comes over and breathes in, "So they were here too. That is not good."

I look at him, "Why? I mean, I have ideas why but I don't know her and she hasn't been great to me so my perception may be uh, skewed."

Father Neally sighs, "Lacey doesn't like most other magical practitioners. As you noticed. She was okay with

Alena because she didn't see her as a magical practitioner. Most of the witches here in town would agree. That is why she lives here instead of near other witches. Ok, we should get out of here and meet up tomorrow night. We aren't going to accomplish more without stepping back to think things through. And, some of us need sleep."

We exit her house quietly, leaving everything mostly untouched. At the street we all split to head to our homes. I get to walk between Scarlet and Leonidas. It's really nice, to feel so loved the feeling is, in some ways, alien to me. I tell them both how I love and appreciate them as we walk home, because I don't ever want them to feel even a portion of how unwanted I always felt before this life happened.

Five

Jasmine

After Scarlett and Leonidas go to their rooms I call to Hekate. She appears almost immediately. We seat ourselves in the chairs she left last time she visited this room and she asks, "What is troubling you dear one?"

"Books. There were three books stolen from the library. We found out tonight, when the spiders started pounding on the door."

She carefully sets her hands on the arms of her chair, "Tell me everything."

I tell her the whole story, leaving nothing out. She blanches when I get to the titles. After telling her about Frank and Lacey's disappearance I say, "Father Neally," her brow raises at his name but she says nothing and I file it away for future reference, "says that we must get those books back. The fate of the world depends on it. Is he right?"

She sighs, "He is right but also underestimating the situation. They are so much more dangerous than he knows. But he wouldn't know. We didn't tell anyone. Of course, we thought when we each hid our books in very different lands that there was no way they would end up in the same building either, yet here we are. I need a drink. You should have a drink too." She holds her hands out and two rocks glasses appear, one in each hand. A golden liquid fills them halfway. She hands one to me and takes a swig from her own.

I sip and liquid gold runs down my throat, "What is this? It is amazing."

She eyes me, "Nothing you should ever admit to having. Leave it at that."

My eyes go round and I nod, "Sure thing. Expensive booze. Got it."

She chuckles, "Good. We have enough problems with the books. I am sure it is difficult to believe but even the gods are born and have to grow up. We have the added complication of having a magnificent amount of power that we tend to grow into long before the maturity to handle it has grown in. Some of us go through a troubled time, much like humans. Persephone, Anubis, myself. Each of us had our own problems and we wrote things down. Unfortunately, we were incautious in what we wrote. If a spell popped into our minds we wrote it down. When that much emotion is put into a set of writings they sort of take on a life of their own. None of us wanted to destroy our creations. Even after we found out the harm they could cause. We thought that we were powerful gods, we would hide them and they would stay hidden. Ha!"

She sips from her glass and I take the opportunity to ask, "Would they still be living? After all this time?"

Hekate shrugs, one shoulder lifting briefly, "Possibly? We hid them so long ago and none of us have touched any of them in at least that long. I would like to think the life in them had faded to nothing by now, but I cannot be certain."

"Would any of the guardians have been able to tell?"

She looks over at me, "Possibly. If they paid them any attention. If they examined it with power. Or psychic sight. But the chances of anyone doing that to a book are slim. These books, they don't just have the capability to end this world. They could end all of them."

Taking in her words I down the rest of my drink. "All of them. As in all the worlds in this solar system?"

Hekate glares at me, "If that was what I meant I would have said that. I meant all the worlds in all the systems in this universe."

The glass slips from my hands to the floor with a thunk, so loud in the silence. Fuck me. That's a lot. If we don't get those books back... this planet and all the rest of them are done for. "So failure is not an option, is it?"

"I'm afraid not. And if I am correct about why this happened, I will be restricted in the help I can give you."

"What? But I need you! I am way to much of a fuck up to be let loose to save an entire universe!"

She waves a hand at me, "Pfft. You are so much more capable than you believe you are. I have faith in you and so should you." She leans forward and stretches her arm toward me, her hand cupping my chin, "You will be the most magnificent, kind, and powerful creature to walk this place as guardian. Stay the course and keep faith in yourself that you can handle whatever comes your way."

"I will. I'm not sure why you think I'm worthy of this, I can't see it. But I will do as you say."

She pats the side of my face lightly, "Good. Now I must go. You may call on me at any time, but keep in mind that the physical help I can give currently is almost none."

I nod as she disappears and then whisper, "Thank you." A soft breeze wraps around my shoulders and feels so much like a hug from my mother that I can't stop the fat tears from rolling down my face.

Six

Evening arrives to find me watching the sun go down from the chair I was in when Hekate left. My thoughts were racing all day and my chances of getting rest were zero, so I just stayed here. Besides, vampires don't really need sleep. We just enjoy it. Or at least I do. Wait, maybe the ones that have sun issues need sleep? I don't know. It doesn't matter right now. Maybe if I can manage to save everything I will try to find out. If not, well, it wasn't that important anyway.

I hear people arriving so I rise from my chair and change my clothing. My shoes are where they should be and I am pleased to have this one thing going right. So pleased that I create a tiny little tea set with Earl Grey tea, honey, and the tiniest scones I have ever seen and leave it next to my shoes as my way of saying thanks. I hear a rustling as I leave the closet but I just keep walking so as not to spook it or cause another shoe disappearance.

I find everyone waiting in the kitchen. I know it will be a long damn day and I am going to go ahead and start it with booze and blood because why the fuck not. I can feel everyone watching me as I pour a good amount of whisky in a glass and stir in some blood. Taking a swig from the glass I turn around and lean against the counter, "I spoke with Hekate last night."

Leonidas purses his lips and asks, "Would anyone else like a drink before we hear about this?"

Father Neally is first to say, "I would." The rest of the room follows suit.

While Leonidas prepares drinks my mind wanders and I can't help but notice that Sebastian hasn't been here in days. I wonder if he changed his mind? I have bigger things to worry about right now, and he could just be out of town. I finish my drink as Leonidas passes out the drinks to everyone else. He walks over to stand next to me and hands me a fresh one. Will I ever get used to a man that treats me like a person? I don't know but I am damned well going to give it my best. "Thank you. The good news is she really agrees that we must get these books back now. Yesterday even. The real damned bad news is that it is so much worse than we could have imagined. So much."

Father Neally downs his drink, "How much worse?"

"The universe. This entire fucking universe could go poof if we don't get those books back and they figure out some things."

Father Neally heaves himself up out of his chair and walks over to the cabinet with the booze. Taking down the vodka he looks over at me, "I'll buy you another." Then he flips the cap clean off the bottle and starts chugging it straight from the bottle. When it is completely emptied he carefully picks up the cap and places both cap and bottle in the garbage before he sits back down. "I had no idea that books capable of destroying the entire damn universe were just shelved in the library. I would have been a lot more vigilant about the security."

I nod, "When we get them back we should start with that. Before we leave them unattended in the library we should have it so much more secure. I had a thought while I was watching the sun come up. Can we get some wolves to track Lacey and Frank? I feel like their sense of smell is going to be so much better than ours and I can glamour them so that they appear to the rest of the world as large dogs." Looking at Leonidas I ask, "Do you think they would go for it?"

He shrugs, "Maybe not for me but they definitely would for you and the universe. Let me call Banner." He plants a kiss on my cheek and leaves the room pulling his phone out of his pocket.

"If that is a no go, can we do some kind of locator spell? To find Frank and Lacey?" While Nia and I talk about locator spells Father Neally is focused on the conversation. He nods occasionally, minute but still a nod. His behavior really makes me wonder just how he is part of this library thing. I have a feeling that he isn't just a shifter with a passion for religion.

Leonidas walks in, "Banner says he would be happy to help. He can meet us there as soon as I message him to come."

Father Neally stands, "Perfect. The sun is down now, lets do this."

Seven

We start with Frank's place, just because that was where we started last night. Banner wanders up already in wolf form, he is gorgeous. Black with silver shot throughout his fur and it is so fluffy looking, I can't help it. I kneel down to eye level with him because I have to at least ask, "Banner, can I pet you? I know you aren't—" before I can finish he is nearly in my lap shoving his head under my hand and his fur is luxurious. So soft and silky, I scratch behind his ears and along his back as he makes all these cute noises.

Then he rolls on to his back so I can scratch his belly and Leonidas says, "Ok, that's enough of that. Banner, you have no shame do you?"

Banner jump to his feet and gives us a wolfish grin along with one short bark. I stand and pat his head one last time, "Let's go in now."

We open the door much the same as last night except we let Banner go first and then we stay in the entry area with the door closed so his neighbors don't begin to wonder more about what the fuck we are doing here. A window shatters in the living area and something thumps on the carpet. With the window broken we can hear voices outside. Holy shit, Frank has some amazing soundproofing going in this place. As we are peeking into the living area Banner runs into the entry and shifts, he is very naked and also very distracting, especially once he says, "Guys, Frank's body just appeared in the bedroom under the bed while I was in there."

Father Neally looks back from the living area, "What? Frank's dead?" Banner shakes his head yes. He pokes his head back into the living area and appears to be listening. When he turns back to us he says, "This is bad."

Eight

We hear the sounds of shifters howling drifting in through the broken front window. It almost sounds like they are saying come out. Father Neally says, "They are saying we murdered Frank. They want our heads."

Leonidas slips off to the other room with an unbroken window and is back almost immediately, "There are at least twenty out there, probably more that we don't see."

Scarlett, standing next to me, grabs my arm. "We can't take that many. I'm not ready to go. You have to do something with your magic. You and Nia. Do something." She gives my arm a little push toward Nia.

Nia raises a brow at me and I shrug. She is right, there are only seven of us here, taking on shifters who are about equal in strength with larger numbers is suicide. Father Neally has been cooking his brain on high for the past few minutes looks up and says "Follow me!" He takes off through the house and Scarlett is hot on his heels, leaving the rest of us to follow. We get out of the entry and hear glass shattering in other rooms. Snarls and barks as we run for the doorway. Father Neally is holding the door open and he shouts, "Come on! They're right behind you!"

Leonidas grabs me up and puts on even more speed, diving through the door with me held tightly to him even as he angles us so he takes the brunt of our landing. I hear the door slam shut and a body hit the door hard. I can feel Nia working her magic as I roll off Leonidas and ask him, "Are you okay?"

He laughs, "Yes, I am fine. Vampire, remember? Most things won't hurt us for too long."

Chuckling at his humor I look around, we are back in the library. Awesome. I turn my head to watch the last of Nia's spell and the door we came through disappears from the library.

"I guess now we know what happened to Frank. But why are we being set up for it?" No one really has an answer and I didn't expect one. Getting to my feet brings Scarlett into view, so I go to her and sit in the chair next to her, "Are you ok?"

She draws a shaky breath, "Yeah. Or I will be. I was just really scared for a minute you know? I have a fear of shifters, this didn't really help."

"Oh shit, I don't guess it did. We should get you home. So you can have a long, hot bath and a drink and just forget all of this."

Her smile is gorgeous and sad, "That sounds really perfect."

Nodding once, I stand and tell everyone else, "Hey, I am going to take Scarlett back to the house. It is safe, right?"

Father Neally smiles oddly, "That house is very safe. She will have nothing to fear in that house."

I don't know what that is about so I ignore. Bigger fries and all that. I slip Scarlett's arm through mine and I walk her to the door to the house and I just leave it open while I walk her to her room and run a bath for her. I call in her favorite brandy, bottle and cup. She is in the tub and soaking before I head back to the library. She looks relaxed and soothed, so I won't worry since she is safe at the house.

Back in the library I overhear Father Neally telling someone that the house really is quite safe, it holds the main door for the library and it is really very heavily warded. I walk around a shelf to see Leonidas nodding, his back to me. "Now we need to figure out who killed Frank. Banner, any leads from the house?"

Banner, now with a blanket around his hips and still completely distracting, shrugs, "Yes. But you won't like it. It smelled like the magic from Mikael's house."

Nia says, "We should peek through the door. Lacey's door. We obviously walked into a trap at Frank's house. They had to have known we were there. Possibly that we had been there prior. If it is nothing good we can just slam it and disconnect that one too."

Father Neally presses his lips into a thin line. "You're right. And I don't recall the door being at Lacey's house, now that I think about it. Let's do it now. Better now than later."

We all go over to the door. Father Neally opens it slowly, keeping his body behind the door as it he pulls it wider. The first thing I see as he moves back is char. On the wall, on the floor; I recognize them. I recognize the walls. I stood on that floor and I watched Mikael turn to ashes as his body burnt from the fire I caused. I can hear voices through the door, a whisper leaves my throat, "I'll never be free of him. Never. He is always going to be there. Always fucking up my life. I turned him to ashes, why can't he just go away already?" My fingers tingle with power, I need to find him, to find some way to put an end to all of this.

Leonidas puts his arms around my body, clamping my hands down at my sides and speaking softly in my ear, "Hey, hey, you are here with me. You are safe. It isn't Mikael. That is just where he died, nothing more. He isn't there. I promise. I kicked his ashes myself. You are safe." He just keeps repeating his words till the tingles in my hands recede and I can see more than the char on the walls again. Inhale, shuddering exhale. My eyes open again, everyone is watching me. If it was possible for me to blush I would be doing it right now. Everyone saw me freaking out. I don't even understand why I did that.

In a whisper I tell Leonidas, "I'm ok now. Thank you." He nods and kisses my forehead. I don't deserve that right now but I let it pass. "Sorry about that, just had a moment. What did I miss?"

Father Neally clears his throat, "We all have moments, no apologies needed. We heard Lacey speaking to someone about a mob. That was enough for us and we closed the door. It has been removed and Lacey's access revoked."

"That's good. Very good. So, I guess Lacey is working with the witch from Mikael's place. That's wonderful." I sit down on the floor, "This is all so ridiculous."

Nine

Leonidas lifts Jasmine and takes her to a quiet corner of the library. She makes me wish... Things are too complicated for that. I turn to Nia and Caden, "We need to figure out how long these two have been working together. Is this why Lacey has been so against other magic users?"

Caden shrugs, "I always thought she was just a nasty sort of personality but it is a plausible explanation. She could have been a plant."

Nia sits on a nearby table, "I think there are more important questions to be answered. How many times were they in the library on whatever mission they had? What is their end game? How did they get the door moved without anyone noticing? Did they notice the door being gone yet and if not, how long before they do? Do they need more from the library? Will they target one of us next?"

Banner speaks up from his seat, "To add to that, Why kill

Frank? And more importantly, how are you going to convince the shifter community that the lot of you are not responsible? I can vouch for you, but I don't know how far that will go. Frank was not pack to me and different packs don't always trust each other easily."

The wolf's eyes stray back to Jasmine as soon as he stops speaking, I don't blame him, I have to fight the urge myself. I guess he wants his status kept quiet? "Now that we know the questions, any ideas on how we find the answers? Jasmine recognized that place, and you seemed to know it as well, Banner?"

Banner's eyes focus on me, "Yes. That was Mikael's house. Jasmine killed him literally right there. That is what all the scorch marks came from. She had the reaction because they had a long history and he was trash. We can find the place for sure. But, it is a fuckin' pain to attack if they know you are coming. Try to avoid that."

"If they know? What? Why would you let them know?"

"We didn't let him know, he was the one that turned her too. So he was able to keep tabs on her because of that bond and well, he knew she was powerful so he prepared."

"I see. She chose to kill him or she was forced to kill him?"

Banner leans forward in his chair, "You've met her. How are you even asking that?"

Putting my hands up in a placating gesture I say, "Calm down. I needed to check that my thoughts were accurate."

He leans back in the seat, "She did everything in her power to avoid killing him. Everything. He would have been dead a lot quicker had I any say in the matter. Hell, if she had let Leonidas have any say. It was her wish for us not to kill him that kept him alive."

"I would like to hear that story sometime. One question answered at least. Nia, I seem to recall there being a spell or two that would allow you to see someone's relatively recent past. See if you can find that and figure out some of the reasons why. As for you and Caden and your doors, I would prefer to disconnect those doors for now and I would like for you both to stay either here in the library or, if Jasmine is amenable, at her place. What are your thoughts on this?"

Caden growls, "I don't like it. I am going to do it because I think it is a good idea. I just don't like it. And I will stay here in the library. I don't want to stay in that house. It damn near hums with magic noise plus that fucking creature in the walls wants me dead."

Nia laughs, "You shouldn't have been so rude to Alena. They never forget and forgiveness takes a lot. I will stay here in the library as well. That way, if it is attacked again, there will be two of us here."

"I like that. Will you get those doors disconnected and possibly use your magic to bring Caden's and your things here?" Nia agrees as she hops off the table and heads for her own door. "Caden, I would appreciate it greatly if you and Nia could work out what books they have been reading, if there are any others."

Caden sniffs, "There are no other books missing."

Narrowing my eyes at him I say, "I said what other books they may have read. This is a library. They very well could have read other books and brought them back so as to keep us from noticing they were gone. Lacey could have been checking books out for them for months."

"Oh. Well. Yes. We will definitely work on that."

I hear Banner snickering, but he is very carefully not looking at any of us.

Ten

HAKE

Lacey has told me at least ten times today how much she doesn't like other witches and how I am different. I quit fighting my eyes about rolling every time she says that this morning. Now, I begin to think they will roll right to the back of my skull and refuse to come out until she leaves. I let her drone on though, as long as she is talking she isn't paying any attention to what I am actually doing. She still thinks that idiot wolf is alive and just went home for a while. He was too suspicious and his death was the perfect way to frame Jasmine with his clan.

Trying to avoid being killed by them should buy me enough time to put all my plans in action. Then Jasmine will be mine, I will be immortal, and I will never have to listen to Lacey's prattle ever again.

Lacey's monologue cuts off as she gasps, "It's gone!"

I look to where she is pointing and the door to the

library is gone, as if it were never there. Lacey holds up the key in her hand and it disappears before our eyes. "So, they know that the door was moved. And they have revoked your access. That's fine. We have the books we need. This just moves up the time table. Come, we have components to collect."

Jasmine

I know Mikael is dead. I know he is. I watched his body burn. Seeing the library door open into that house, that spot. Seeing that connection, this new world I live in and the one I ripped out of my life, that wound is fresh again. Raw in a way that I didn't feel when it initially happened. Plus, I have this irrational fear that he is going to come back. That I will never be rid of him. Always looking over my shoulder. Always waiting for his eyes to be watching me again. To be fighting for ownership of myself again.

I just want to move forward from this. I want to live a different life than what he wanted for me.

Leonidas comes to sit on my bed, "How are you holding up? Is there anything I can do for you?"

I look up at him, he is so beautiful. His dark hair and skin darkened lately by the sun he near worships, the way he watches everything. Taking it all in. I know what I want. But can I ask for help? Should I trust him? What if he breaks my heart and I destroy the world about it? I look into his eyes and for all that he spent a lot of his life a gang leader and murderer, all I can see is a man that would burn the world down for me if I needed the warmth. If I can't take a chance on him, then who? Who would ever be good enough? "Could you just hold me? I don't really want or need anything. But I would like to be held."

"Whatever you want love," he tells me as he strips off his jacket and lays down beside me, gathering me into his arms and holding me close. I can smell his scent surrounding me. Mostly leather and cardamom with a hint of cloves. I snuggle in and close my eyes.

Eleven

JASMINE

I slept through the rest of the night and day. When I woke up the sun had set again and Leonidas hadn't moved. When I stirred a bit he made a rumbling noise deep in his chest and said, "A little better now?"

"I am. Thank you for staying with me. For keeping me safe from my nightmares."

He pulls back a little to look me in the eye, "I will always be here for you, however you need me to be. And really, there are much worse ways to spend a night than holding a gorgeous woman close."

"Flattery will get you everywhere sir," I say as I move to press my lips against his. Just as our lips touch I hear a group of people yelling my name outside.

Leonidas groans, "Interrupting assholes. Want me to kill them for you?"

I laugh, "No. Well. Not yet. Let's at least see what they want."

We get up from the bed and wander to the door. These fuckers are yelling for me to come out the entire time. I remember that staying in the house offers a protection we won't have if we step out the door and I caution Leonidas about it. "In here they can't touch us, do not step outside if they act the fool."

That said I open the door and look out at the fools standing on my porch. "Can I help you?"

They stop the interminable shouting and the larger one of them steps forward, "Jasmine Felton, you are commanded to come and face pack justice for the murder of Frank Gatchley."

"Who is it that has decided they get to command me?"

"Pack leader Gentry commands you."

I laugh, "Who the fuck is that? No one has authority over me, I am not beholden to any pack. Nor did I murder Frank. How did you all decide that I was the one that did this? Did you draw my name out of a hat?" He looks confused and I wonder if I spoke too fast for him. "I said, how did you all decide I murdered Frank?"

He looks annoyed, maybe he did understand what I said and was thinking? "We have it from a reliable party that you are the murderer. Now you must come and face pack justice for killing one of ours." He reaches for my arm as he finishes speaking. I watch with amusement because I haven't ever gotten to see what exactly will happen and I have high hopes for shocking results. His hand starts to pass the threshold and I can see the magic race at him. Then he is landing in the yard, looking confused and smoking just a little.

"Man, there is no smell quite so bad as burnt dog hair. My guy, you are going to smell bad for days if you don't go trim it all and have a shower right after. Or don't, I can't tell you what to do."

He growls at me as he stands, "You have to come out sometime witch. We'll be waiting for you."

One of the others standing in the driveways starts howling, "Murderer! She's a murderer!"

Another takes up the cry and adds that I won't be safe anywhere.

I ask the big guy, "So how did Frank die anyway?"

Big guy looks sharply at me, "Don't try me witch! You know very well how he died."

"Honestly, I haven't even seen his body. But, if there is magic on it that doesn't smell like me, it wasn't me. Maybe think about that while you have your pretend trial."

Big guy is silent before turning and walking away. His followers chant a little bit longer, insisting that I will not escape pack justice before they too leave.

***

After that lovely exchange I go find my phone and call Banner. I put it on speaker because I know Leonidas wants to hear the answers too. He answers on the first ring, "Hello gorgeous, hope you are feeling better?"

I can't help but smile as I say, "Well, yes and no. Banner, what exactly is pack justice?"

I hear something clank to the ground, "Nothing you need to worry about, you aren't pack. Where did you hear that term?"

"Some guys showed up saying I had to face pack justice

for Frank's murder. I told them no, but I didn't actually know what I was declining. Could you tell me more about it?"

He chuckles, "Woman, you get into more trouble than any three wolf cubs. Tell you what, we aren't supposed to discuss pack laws with outsiders but I will for you if you finally have that lunch with me?"

Leonidas laughs, "Banner, you asshole."

Banner doesn't miss a beat, "I am good with pack dynamics and she seems to be building one. I told you I would try if there was ever an opportunity."

"You did. And I can't even fault you. Luckily for you, she is the only one with any say over who she sees. I would happily keep her to myself."

Banner laughs, "So, beautiful, what do you say? Come have lunch with me?"

I chew my lip a bit, "I don't know if it would be safe? Those wolves, they said they would get me, that I would have to go outside eventually."

Banner growls, "You will be safe with me. I'll have some of my men come with us. You will not be unguarded."

I look over to Leonidas, silently asking him if he thinks this is a good idea and he nods with a smile. "Ok, I'll go. Where do you want to meet?"

"I'll pick you up at your place and bring you back there. That way you will have escort the entire time."

"Perfect. Where are we going?"

"A little magic place, they have great steaks for me and a wide selection of bloods ethically sourced for you. They have donors from various races, apparently they all taste different."

"Nice, it isn't fancy or anything, right?"

"Nah. Your life is complicated enough without that.This

place is average. Great food but casual dress. Pick you up in two hours?"

"Yes. See you then!"

I end the call and Leonidas takes me in his arms, "Perhaps now we can finish what we started?" His lips touch mine and fire lights up every nerve ending as I press my body against his.

"Jasmine! Why does it smell like burnt wolf up in here?" Scarlett calls out at the worst possible time.

Leonidas groans, "We roasted wolf this morning for interrupting. Don't worry about it."

The door to my bedroom opens, Scarlett standing there with a grin, "Aw, poor thing. Am I interrupting you too? Seriously, Jas, why is the place rank with burnt wolf hair?"

Giving Leonidas one more quick kiss I step back and head for the door while he throws himself on my bed with a groan. "The wolves came by and one of them tried to snatch me out of the house. He found out that the house doesn't let go of what belongs here so easily."

Scarlett follows me to the kitchen, "The wolves?What wolves and why did they try to snatch you?"

"It was Frank's pack. Something about some pack justice for Frank's murder. I am going to find out more from Banner in a little while when he picks me up to go to lunch."

"Is that really safe? I mean, you have this unknown witch teamed up with Lacey after you and now wolves. Is going out to lunch really a great idea when you are safe here?" Scarlett seats herself at the table in the kitchen while I hop up to sit on the counter.

Shrugging I say, "He said that he would have his guys with us to guard. Leonidas, what guys does he have? I never asked."

Leonidas never moves from my bed as he answers, "He is a pack alpha. He has his own damn pack. He could theoretically call the whole damn pack to protect you while you go to lunch. That is part of why I agreed that it wouldn't be terrible for you to go out with him. It brings more protection for you."

"Fuck. I had no idea. Ok. Well there you go Scarlett. I am sure I will be well protected."

"Really? What if Banner and Frank are from the same pack?"

Leonidas yells from my bedroom, "They are not the same pack! You know very well they aren't the same pack."

Scarlett looks embarrassed so I just let it go. "I'll be fine. Really. Don't worry about me, everything will work out and we will finally have a nice quiet life for at least a few decades."

Scarlett looks up at me, "Will we? How can you be sure? It seems like danger follows you harder than your shadow."

Her tone and the serious set to her face scare me, "What's this about Scarlett? Is there something we need to talk about?"

She looks hard at me in silence for long moments before saying, "It's nothing. It has just been a weird few days and I am unsettled."

I hop down and walk over to her, kneeling next to her chair and hugging her close. Her arms slip around me and she sighs. "I'm sorry Scarlett. I have been wrapped up in my head and I didn't think to ask how you were doing. How you were holding up in all this. Is there anything I can do to help? To reassure you?"

She pulls away, "No. I just need to get my act together. I'll be fine."

They way she pulled away kind of hurt but I don't want to make her feel bad so I put on a bright smile and keep my hands to myself, "Well, if you need anything, I am here for you. Just let me know," I tell her as I stand and move to lean against a counter.

She nods, "I will, if there is anything you can do. I think I am going to go visit Chloe, I haven't seen her in a minute. Her and Eason have been jetting all over the place."

"I know. It is so sweet. I love how happy they seem."

Sorrow flashes across Scarlett's face so fast I think I could have imagined it, "It is. I am really happy for her. I'll see you later." She leaves, moving fast out the door. I feel a sinking feeling in my heart but I push it aside for now and head for my bedroom. Not much time left before Banner shows up.

Twelve

JASMINE

Banner arrives in an SUV that seems a little over the top for a lunch. But then I get in the front seat and see that there are four other wolves in here with me besides Banner as he gets into the driver's seat. He reintroduces me to Dario and Mario, and introduces me to Denton and Elliot. They are all really quite nice and we chat on the way. Soon enough we pull into the parking lot of what looks like a small eatery but smells like magic. The men in the back get out before the SUV is fully stopped.Two stand at either end of the SUV and wait, while the other two go inside the eatery.

I get out and Banner is quickly at my side, as we step onto the sidewalk the two that remained at the truck fall in behind us. This level of caution feels unreal even if I understand why it's necessary. We are seated in a spot near the windows which were opaque from the outside but provide a great view from inside. The four men that came with us sit two to a table on either side of us. So we have privacy but I am still protected. Our server is the most adorable woman.

She maybe stands five feet tall and she has round, voluptuous curves everywhere. At the same time she is, I think, one of the fae. So she has this ethereal look about her, otherworldly. Her voice could give sirens a run for their money.

Banner is amused at my preoccupation with Silvie, and for her part Silvie thinks I am sweet and Banner should shut his hole. I like her more now. She gives us menus and tells me that she will be back as soon as I set the menu on the table. I thank her and check out the menu. While our menus appear exactly the same from the outside, his is tailored to wolves and mine to vampires. He was right about the variety of blood at this place. All I have ever tried is human so I read all the descriptions very carefully before deciding to try siren. I doubt sincerely that I will ever run into one that I want to drain so, why not try it here?

I set my menu down and Silvie appears next to us. "Decided what you want?"

"I would like to try the siren. It sounds relatively safe for me as I haven't tried well, anything not a regular human."

"It is. It is one of the much tamer types we have here, good choice. And for you sir?"

Banner tells her that he wants a large steak, slightly seared and a sweet tea. She nods, tells us they will be out soon and is gone again.

I feel eyes on me but, we are out in public. I look around as surreptitiously as possible but I don't see anyone focusing on me. I shrug it off and ask Banner, "So, pack justice. Why does that not apply to me?"

"Because you aren't pack. Literally, you aren't part of any pack. No pack can enforce pack justice on someone outside of the pack hierarchy. The fact that they tried to do that is...

not good for their pack. Outside of a singular pack there are further hierarchies, packs that other packs answer to, as part of keeping things under wraps."

"What does that mean? Do you all have a bureaucracy?"

"Hmm, of a sort, yes. We have individual packs, familial packs that can encompass multiple individual packs, state leaders, regional leaders, and over all that is the royal family."

"Royalty? Fancy. Where do you fall in all this?"

He looks uncomfortable as he says, "I am a regional leader of sorts…"

"Of sorts?" I tip my head to one side, "What does of sorts mean?"

He looks down, "It means I took the role because I didn't want the one I was born to and will eventually have to accept. Oh, look, food is here!"

He seems so happy that the food is here and I decide not to push about what exactly he was born to, for now. His plate is set in front of him and he inhales deeply, a quiet rumble of appreciation rolling in his chest. The rumble does things to me that make his eyes flash as he scents the arousal in me. Silvie sets a delicate glass filled with blood that smells of desire and something else that I can't quite place in front of me. I haven't fed at all today and I am very hungry with this in front of me.

I wait long enough for Silvie to disappear and I pick up the glass as Banner starts eating. Bringing it to my lips I tip the glass and drink deeply. I didn't know until now that desire had a flavor or that it would make me burn? My body suddenly feels wrong. I set the glass down and look at Banner through eyes that aren't focusing, "Banner, I think…"

My tongue is thick and isn't working so great, "I think something is wrong."

My body is burning up from the inside as Banner grabs my cup and brings it to his nose. He barks orders at his men and Silvie is there, I see her lead two of the men to the kitchen after giving Banner a cup with a lid. I can barely hold myself up and Banner scoops me up as I start to lean. My eyes close and darkness welcomes me.

Banner

Fuck. Fuck. Fuck. I talk her into an outing with the promise of safety and she is poisoned right in front of me. "Shut them up! But don't kill them yet." The two that tainted her siren blood are trussed up in the back, struggling and making too much racket. Jasmine is in and out as I race to her house. Wolf healers would do her no good and are more likely to feel like one less vampire is all for the good. But I can't let her die. I've needed to be closer to her since the first day I scented her.

She can't die right as I start to get near her. Her house looms and almost feels like it is pulling us closer. I screech to a halt in front, slamming it into park before running to pull her out of the SUV, "Take those two and lock them up. I'll let you know what will happen to them after we know what has happened to her." I am walking in the house as the last of that leaves my lips but I have no doubt they heard me as I hear doors slam and the vehicle pull away. "Scarlett!"

She darts into the living area where I am pacing, "Oh gods, no. What happened?"

I quickly explain to her about the blood and how it was tainted.

Scarlett's eyes go round as saucers, "I don't know anyone that has ever come through that." Red tears runs down her face as she runs a finger along Jasmine's face. "Wait. Father fucking Neally. That old bastard knows shit and so does the elf." She sniffles as she whips out her phone and taps the screen before putting it to her ear, "She's been poisoned with wolf blood."

I can hear Father Neally huffing as he tells her get to the library door, he will open it from the other side and to get her in there now. I am moving before the words finish coming from his mouth. I remember where the door is from the other night and I could find it by smell anyway. He opens the door as I get to it and I walk in with Scarlett hot on my heels.

"She should never have gone out in public right now, this is your fault wolf!" Scarlett is as charming as ever and points out things I am well aware of, things I will torture myself with later if she doesn't survive. Father Neally sends everything on a large table flying across the room with one sweep of his arm and tells me to lay her down there.

Thirteen

Scarlett is still yelling at me as I snatch my shirt off to form a pillow for Jasmine. Father Neally looks to her and says, "Blood, bring all you have. Leave the door open while you fetch it." She disappears into the house and he looks at me, "You didn't see this." I nod as he uses magic to call books to himself and I can't help but wonder just what the old man is.

He calls in an IV setup and runs his hands over the books he called to himself. He selects one and sends the others back with a wave of his hand. Scarlett zips in, a large cooler in her hands and Leonidas behind her. Scarlett notices the IV setup and gets it hooked to Jasmine, fresh blood coursing into her veins.

Father Neally asks, "How was she poisoned?"

"It was mixed in with siren's blood in a glass. She drank half the glass before she realized something was wrong."

Father Neally frowns and runs off to another part of the library, coming back with another book open as he runs. He flips pages like mad before shouting, "Aha! Elf blood. We need elf blood and she just might survive it." His phone is out and he taps the screen then sets it on the table next to Jasmine. I hear the elf answer, "Father Nea-"

He cuts her off, "No time. Get in to the library, Jasmine's poisoned and we need your blood to save her."

Nia runs in with the phone still pressed to her ear. Stopping next to Father Neally she holds out her arm, but he says, "Look at this," and he catches her up on the problem.

Jasmine is starting to whimper and thrash in pain, Leonidas and I step forward to keep her from injuring herself or the ones that might save her, holding her as gently as possible.

Nia presses her lips together, "I don't know if we have caught it in time."

Some god in a lot of robe and hood appears in the library at the same time as an incredibly fierce looking goddess that can only be Jasmine's Hekate. The god smiles in his shadows, "It would take so little to push her over the edge."

The woman smiles and I nearly shit myself. She is terrifying as she tells him, "Do it. Then I will no longer be bound by the rules." With the exception of Jasmine, everyone is frozen in fear, she glances at us and hisses, "Carry on as if we are not here! Now!"

Nia cuts her hand and lets her blood flow into a bowl. When the amount she wants is in the bowl she binds her wound quickly before whispering a spell to put her blood into the bag feeding into Jasmine's arm. Father Neally takes Nia's hand and they both whisper a spell over Jasmine. Even I can see the magic flow over her and settle in as the two in the corner look on. All the blood has entered her from the bag and Father Neally disconnects the IV. Jasmine is thrashing and crying out in pain. The wolf in me is straining to get to her until I cannot fight it any longer. I shift and jump onto the table next to her as she cries out and her body curls into a ball, shimmering briefly and then a black wolf lays panting on the table in place of Jasmine. I look to the two in the corner as Hekate laughs, loud and long. The other scowls and fades into the shadows. I lay down beside her as Father Neally looks to Hekate, "What does this mean?"

Hekate smiles fierce and... proud? "My Jasmine has gained another power instead of dying." She looks at me, "If she hasn't changed again when she wakes up, make her shift."

Leonidas clears his throat and Hekate raises a brow at him. "Sorry to interrupt, I have a question that I think is important. Will her bite kill us now? Will she still be a vampire? Will our bite kill her?"

Hekate laughs, "That would be awkward now wouldn't it? Certainly put a damper on some activities. But no. She is a different creature now. She will need food and blood to survive." She looks at Jasmine, her eyes shining, "She is exactly where I hoped she would be though some will call her abomination. There has never been one like her and it isn't likely there ever will be again. What she is cannot be transmitted, not through bite or sex or any other way. This was thousands of years of work culminating, banking on her survival. Guard her well till she is recovered." Hekate fades into nothing and I lay my head down next to Jasmine, to wait for the change in her breathing.

Fourteen

LEONIDAS

I should probably feel some jealousy that Banner lays on the other side of Jasmine but I can't. His presence seems more a comfort for me as I know he would do anything to protect her. I set my hands into her fur and just rest them there, content to feel her breathe. To feel her heart beat.

Scarlett stands farther away from the table Jasmine is on as she says, "Now what?"

Father Neally glances at her and sits on the table across from Jasmine. His glamour drops as Jasmine changes under my hands. I don't look down and give her away as Scarlett shouts, "What in the hell? Who the fuck are you?"

He chuckles and says, "Father Neally?" Nia laughs and he shrugs, "Once, a very long time ago, Demetris of Phaleron."

Scarlett pales, "Demetris? The Demetris? Commissioned to create the Library of Alexandria Demtris?"

He nods, a grim set to his mouth, "Oddly enough, there were some gods that were not happy about the creation of the library. They decided that the fool that carried out the orders should stay to guard it. Forever."

Nia makes a noise, "Oh Demetris, such a punishment for following orders."

He chuckles, "I feel grateful not to have been one of the Ptolemy's that did the ordering. Their punishment was so much worse."

Scarlett scoffs, "Poor thing, had to live forever and guard what you made. You still haven't answered my question, now what? What do we do with her now that she is this?" She gestures vaguely in Jasmine's direction and I feel my lip curl back over my teeth even as I hear Banner growling.

Demetris looks at Jasmine and sees she is watching. He says, "I imagine we will need to ask her what she wants done with her. She's awake if you want to have a go at it, I would have a care how I did that if I were you. Her guardians don't seem to appreciate your assessment of the situation."

***

Jasmine

I ask him, "Does this mean you are done hiding yourself Father Neally?"

He chuckles, "You can call me Demetris. It will be nice to use my first name again. Yes, Father Neally is done now. I will not pretend him any longer beyond tying the loose ends of his life before he leaves and is never seen again."

"Why did you keep your identity a secret from us? Why leave us in the dark when you could have explained so much?"

He rolls his shoulders, "Sometimes it is nice to not be *the* Demetris of Phaleron. The one the put together the Library of Alexandria. The one cursed by the God of Death himself, ironic as his wife has a book in here. You are, most of you, new to this world. But some of you," he looks at Nia and Scarlett, "have been around long enough that you know my name. You recognize it and have expectations. Even those of you that are new would have quickly done research or asked around and found out. The weight of it is a burden that I occasionally like to set down. But, I have set it down for long enough. Some could argue that I set it down for too long." He smiles ruefully, "They would be right. But it is done now. I will be here to aid you and guide you as you need or wish, without the deception of Father Neally's persona."

I work at sitting up and realize that I have been laying here naked. Super. I call in a blanket and wrap it round me, "Well, now that's all cleared up, who wants to help me catch up on what happened after I drank the siren's blood. Did I have a bad reaction to it? Is that why I am on a table in the library? And why don't I have any clothing?"

Scarlett looks incredulous and says, "You turned into a fucking wolf. That's what happened. A fucking wolf. You know wolf bites, shifter bites of any kind are poison to vampires? As is their blood? You are fucking poison now!"

Leonidas snarls at her, "You heard Hekate as well as I did, she said that isn't the case here. Stop twisting things to suit your fear!"

"Fuck you!" she screams at him, "I don't give a damn what anyone says, I have seen shifter blood kill vampires.

The same way it nearly killed her!" She points a finger at me, "And maybe it would have been better if we had let nature take its course. Now she is a danger to everyone."

Leonidas' hands are digging into the table behind me as he speaks in a low voice, "That is the last time you spew any of those lies or it will be your last time able to speak ever because I will cut your tongue out in a way that it won't grow back."

She hisses at him, "Fucking try it, I'll rip your damn head off."

I reach up and unleash a thunderclap in the library by snapping my fingers, silence ensues and I tell them, "Stop fighting. We all need to calm down and take a minute to adjust. Scarlet, I love you and I would never do anything to hurt you, I hope you know that."

She is silent for so long I think she won't answer. She does, saying, "I do know that. I think, I think I need some time to process this. I am going to go to our house. No one is there right now, Chloe is with Eason in some other country." She never looks at me as she leaves the library, walking on the shattered pieces of my heart as she goes.

Fifteen

Jasmine

Banner has been helping me learn how to navigate being a wolf in the week since I was poisoned. He is back today for our next outing but I just want to sit here on my porch. He sits down in the chair opposite me, "Want to talk about it?"

I look down at my hand on the armrest. You can't tell what a messed up mash of things I am from looking at any one part of me and maybe that is part of the problem. I watch him through the veil of my lashes, "Everyone is uncomfortable with me since this happened. Scarlett hasn't been here since, I don't know if things will ever be the same again with her." I choke back a sob, "I don't know if she will ever be willing to even see me again. Leonidas acts like I am fragile and I might break. Sebastian hasn't been here, and I know he has come home. He hasn't answered my calls or messages either."

Banner nods, his face drawn, "Change is hard for everyone. They are probably more worried for you than about you, Leonidas is definitely worried for you. And it is a lot to wrap their minds around. Most people have more problems accepting change and new things as they age, they form habits and want things to stay the same. Give them time to adjust. If it makes you feel any better, I am thrilled. This has given me reason to see you much more than I could if I was just dating you."

Looking at his face all I can see is sincerity, "Really? You aren't put off by," I wave a hand at myself, "all this?"

He chuckles, "Put off is not what I would use to describe what I am in relation to you. Drawn, yes. Turned on, definitely. Continually amazed, absolutely."

"Oh." I hadn't expected any of that.

He stands extending a hand toward me, "Ready to go for a run now?"

The wolf in me perks up at this and I take his hand as I stand, "Yes, I think I am. Thank you Banner."

He gives my hand a squeeze as we walk to the wooded area behind my house.

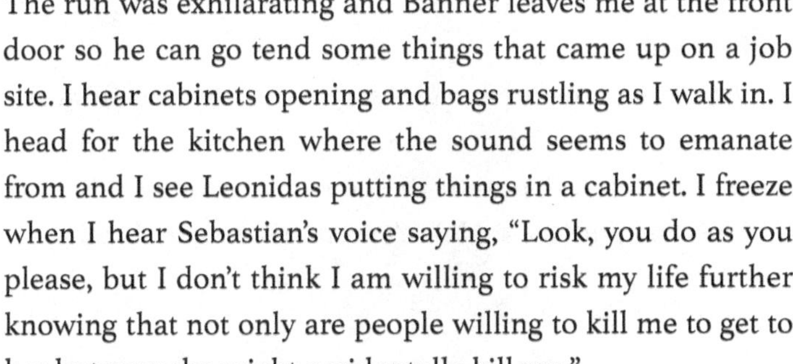

The run was exhilarating and Banner leaves me at the front door so he can go tend some things that came up on a job site. I hear cabinets opening and bags rustling as I walk in. I head for the kitchen where the sound seems to emanate from and I see Leonidas putting things in a cabinet. I freeze when I hear Sebastian's voice saying, "Look, you do as you please, but I don't think I am willing to risk my life further knowing that not only are people willing to kill me to get to her but now she might accidentally kill me."

Scarlett takes up where he left off, "You know it's true Leonidas. She could kill any one of us by accident now. I certainly am not going to trust Hekate to have my best interests at heart, I remember the things she used to get up to before she stopped being so present. People dying has never broken her heart."

Leonidas has been putting things in cabinets all this time and he stills now, "I don't care. If she asked I would burn the damn world down for her, with you in it. I believe Hekate, but even if Jasmine killed me by accident, what a way to go. Why are you here? What reason is there for you both to try to convince me to be like you? Neither of you gives a good goddamn about me."

Scarlett speaks quietly, "Because we are afraid of what she could become, what she could become if we stay, and what she will become when we leave. What will happen when we leave her. We didn't want to leave you here to face the fallout alone with no warning."

I can't stand to hear anymore as my heart shatters again into tiny pieces. I step into the doorway of the kitchen, "You needn't worry about what I will do to you or anyone else. If you are afraid of what I have become or will become, you are free to leave. I would not hold anyone that did not want to... did not... I won't hold you unwilling. I will be fine without you."

I can't look at them, can't stay here. Turning from the kitchen I run. I feel the tears begin to fall as I run and I just keep going. Running until there are no more tears left, till no one is behind me, till I don't even know where I am.

Sixteen

When I stop I am in a wooded area and it is full night. I can see just fine but I don't have the slightest fucking clue where the hell I am or what direction I should go in to find home. I wonder if I have a signal here? I pull my phone out of my back pocket and pull up the map service, but I only have one bar so it is taking forever. It finally shows me where I am in relation to home and fuck. I ran a long damn way. Well, I have a direction anyway so I put my phone back in my pocket and start heading that way.

Not bothering with trying to be fast at getting home, it isn't like I have to worry about the sun coming up. I haven't gone far when two shady looking guys pop up. Scenting the air I can tell they are wolves and that they don't wash as often as they could. The one on the left is stockier, wearing a jean jacket with the sleeves ripped off. His hair is blond and hangs in greasy chunks off his scalp.

His friend shares a stylist with him, only his hair is darker. I can't quite tell the color in the shadows beyond it is darker. He is wearing the filthiest undershirt I have ever seen and I saw quite a few living in the trailer parks.

Blond hair says, "You look lost little lady." He narrows his eyes at me, "Wait a minute! I recognize you! You're the one that killed Frank!" He jostles his darker haired buddy, "Oh, he is going to be happy with us when we bring her home!"

My eyes roll involuntarily, this is my life. I take off for some time alone and this bullshit pops up. "Listen guys, today has not been good. Can we do this on a different day?"

The wolves grin at each other and the one with darker hair says, "Nah. Princess. You are coming with us."

I try one more time because I don't want to be this monster that my lovers are so afraid I'll become, "Guys, I really am not in the mood. If I have to talk to you any further I am going to kill you."

They laugh and it pisses me off. Then the blond one says, "Good luck with that bitch. There's two of us and one of you."

"Do you need to sit down after doing the math in your head like that? I think I smell smoke..." The wolves growl at me and start forward, "I tried to tell you guys." Using my vampire speed I grab the darker haired one and run up a large tree with him. Stopping on a large branch I hold him out over the ground as he strains to grab me, to move me. His attempts are silent as I keep the pressure on his throat. The blond one is still on the ground trying to figure out where we went, I grin at the guy I am holding as I curl the hand holding him into a claw and slowly dig my fingers into his throat. With a shake I rip his throat out and send him crashing through the tree limbs to hit his friend. Dropping the bits left in my hand I rush down the tree and manage to barrel into the blond one shortly after the body of his friend hit him. We land on the ground, me on his chest and I punch his throat, turning it into mush before I give his head a sharp twist, breaking his neck and mostly ripping his head off. I look over at the other and realize he is healing. I am going to have to take their heads all the way off if I want it to stick. I grab the blond head before me and finish snatching it off the body, tossing it away. The other guy is struggling, flopping around, probably trying to breathe. I grab his head and twist hard, ripping it off and throwing it. Looking around me, I can't do anything but shake my head at the blood and the carnage.

I am exactly what they worried I would become. I am the monster they feared. The scream rips out of my throat and hot tears stream down my face. Sobs wrack my body as I wrap my arms around myself, how am I going to live with myself? With this monster I have become? When the tears slow and finally stop the sun is well overhead. I need to get away from here, I'm surprised none of the men's relatives have found them and me out here.

Seeing the dried blood all over my hands I realize that I probably have it on my face too. I think I need to stay in the cover of the woods until dark falls again. Sadly, I don't smell any convenient streams nearby. Standing, I look around to get my bearings. It all looks the fucking same to me so I give up and dig out my phone again. After a wait it points me in the right direction agan and I close the app before I shove the phone back in my pocket and start walking.

Near sunset I finally make it to a road and following it a ways I find a shady looking gas station. I climb a tree set back in the woods a bit and wait for full night to descend.

There haven't been any cars passing by this whole time,

though the lights for the station came on and I can see a clerk in there. Probably a nice quiet place to work. Deciding it is probably as safe to go over there as it will get, I hop down from my perch. I stop inside the tree line and check for cars, other people, and to make sure the clerk is occupied. The place is desolate and the clerk has a magazine and is sitting on a stool. I dash across the road to the side of the store. The door to the women's bathroom is locked so I give it a firm tug as quietly as possible while forcing the knob. It comes open with a minimum of noise, though I don't know if it will ever work quite right again.

The bathroom is dingy and not terribly clean but the sink works. I just need to wash off the blood. Happily, there are paper towels in here. I grab a few and get them wet, using the really awful mirror to clean away all the blood I can see. I have to stop and rinse my hands and arms, I was just getting more blood on myself. After what seems like forever I get myself cleaned up and get the floor cleaned from all the drips. Shifters and CSI would be able to find it but no one else will notice it. Ridiculous how blood spreads like that. Leaving the bathroom I slip around back and avoid the front of the store entirely. The road should lead back into town so I start walking along it.

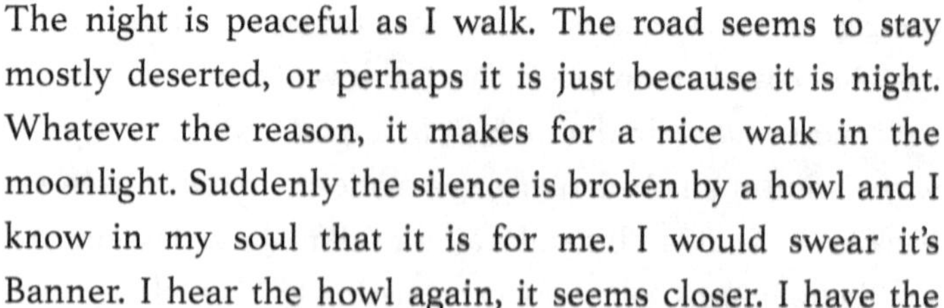

The night is peaceful as I walk. The road seems to stay mostly deserted, or perhaps it is just because it is night. Whatever the reason, it makes for a nice walk in the moonlight. Suddenly the silence is broken by a howl and I know in my soul that it is for me. I would swear it's Banner. I hear the howl again, it seems closer. I have the strongest urge to howl back, but do I want them to see me like this?

Can I handle seeing them? Fuck it. What's the worst that could happen? I tip my head back and howl, "Aar-rrrooooooooo!" I hear him howl back in answer, he sounds excited. Happy? Then I hear so many running through the woods, fuck I hope it was Banner. What if I was wrong? A man and wolves burst out of the woods across the street, stopping to search the darkness. I give a little, "Rooooooo," they turn in my direction as one. I recognize Leonidas and Banner in his wolf form. I don't recognize the other wolves but I feel it is a safe bet they are with them as they all break into a run toward me looking as delighted as I have ever seen a man and a pack of wolves. Which is to say I have never seen this before but they seem happy. I guess if they aren't I'll be dead and won't have this to worry about again. Then Leonidas and a very naked Banner are hugging me hard as the wolves press in against our legs.

Both men are telling me how worried they have been but stop abruptly, exchanging a look. Leonidas asks, "What have you been doing? Why do you have blood all over your clothes?"

I look away, "Fighting. It's what I'm good for. A couple of wolves tried to jump me when I was on my way back. I told them I was in no mood but they didn't want to listen."

Leonidas shakes his head, "Fucking hell Jasmine, come on. Let's get you home before anyone else tries to kill you. Why didn't you answer any of our calls or messages?"

I pull out my phone and show them, I have barely any signal and haven't gotten any messages or calls. "I am sorry. I didn't mean for everyone to be out searching for me. I was on my way home, really."

Banner growls and shifts back to wolf next to me. Leonidas says, "Well, not everyone is out."

I swallow hard around the huge lump in my throat, forcing the words out I say, "Oh. Did they leave already? I didn't know they would be gone so fast."

Leonidas hugs me hard, "Probably. But I am not going anywhere. You are stuck with me, just like I said." He takes my face in his hands and gently turns me to look at him, "I would destroy this world to keep you, the whole damn thing just so you would be safe in it." Banner barks and presses against my side, I drop a hand down to scratch the fur behind his ear as Leonidas adds, "And Banner. I think he means you are stuck with him too. Probably he wouldn't mind helping with the destroying the world part either."

Banner growls in what sounds like assent and I can't help but smile.

Seventeen

"So who has the quill?" Lacey asks for what must be the fifteenth time. Perhaps she thinks the answer will change?

I wonder, "Are you frightened of her? Is that why you keep asking, Lacey?"

She fidgets as she says, "I fear no witch here. And definitely not Edna. She is so goody two shoes that she barely does anything with her magic for fear of accidentally hurting someone with it."

"Then what is the problem Lacey? Why do you keep asking?" I am running out of patience with her. Her inane questions, her evasive answers.

Lacey shrugs, "I have a bad feeling about it. That's all. I keep asking because I hope the answer will change the way I feel about it. Maybe we should wait till she is gone and just steal the quill."

Why couldn't she tell me this before? Moron. Rubbing a

temple with the hand not on the steering wheel I tell her, "Ok. Sure. We can wait until she leaves. Nice to know you have some small amount of precog, any other bad feelings that you haven't mentioned yet?"

My voice rose with each word and by the end she was flinching with each. Not scared of any witch here? I think you have lied to me Lacey. She will bear more watching in the future. She shakes her head no and stares out the window. We are nearly to the witch's house and I pull into a store lot. I cast two spells, one to let us know when the witch leaves her home, the other to make people's eyes slide away from the car. I don't know how long we will need to sit here and it will be easier if we don't have nosy fucks to concern ourselves with. Leaning my seat back I wiggle around a little to get comfortable. Lacey watches as though I have grown another head and plan to eat her with the new one, "You may as well relax. There is no telling how long it will be before she leaves her house. We will wait here till it happens."

"What if I need to go to the bathroom?"

"Then go? I cast a spell to make people's eyes slide away from this spot, so walking back will likely be annoying but you can do it."

"Oh. I guess I will go do that then."

Letting my eyes drift closed I wave a hand at her to encourage her leaving. The silence sounds glorious as she heads for the store.

Some hours later I wake to the spell letting me know the house is empty. Night has fallen and the parking lot is brightly lit. Sitting up I start to reach over and wake Lacey, just before I touch her I stop myself, she is quiet when she is sleeping. Starting the car I drive to the witch's house and pull into the drive. I go straight to the front door as if I belong here and knock. When I don't get an answer I cast a quick glamour to make it appear as though she has answered her door and let me in. Luckily, as Lacey said, she doesn't use her magic much, even for protection of her home. Incredible. I close the door behind me and wander through the house, looking quietly for the quill. I finally find it, just laying on her desk. Like she had been writing letters with this irreplaceable quill.

I am on my way to the front of the house when I hear the door open and close. I back up into shadows and pull them around me. The woman calls out, "I know you are in here. Why are you here?"

I decide to face her, she is probably weak anyway. Stepping out of the shadows I seek her out. She is in her kitchen, making tea of all things. As I walk in she asks, "What did you come here for?"

"I came for a quill."

"Why not knock? I would have gifted it to you."

"No one just gifts magical items to another." Her lies irritate my already frayed nerves. "I am well aware of the lengths you went to in order to have this quill. Why do you women always lie? Own your greed!"

Her face pales, "I would never... I think you should leave sir."

The frightened lady act is giving me hives. Lashing out with my magic I pin her to the wall of her own house. Casting a quick sound-proofing over the entire house I smile. It has been entirely too long since I cut loose and did exactly what I want. Maybe this will make Lacey's voice easier to deal with while I need her around.

The torture of the witch with the quill went much too fast. She died long before I wanted her to, so weak. Lacey never even woke up. Morning was on us by the time we left. We make another two stops at witch supply stores, I send her in so that my face isn't noticed. She picks up the blue ink made of a copper oxide, birch bark paper, some herbs for wrapping around the quill to turn it's purpose to my will. That done, we stop at a museum that has a display that includes a particular cauldron. One that is so much older than they could dream. We tour the museum just to get a look at it. Once in the car again, I simply call it to me. As we drive away I can hear the sound of the alarms going, it is music to my ears.

Unfortunately, this means Lacey is wide awake and telling me her plans. "The library could be so much better. It could be opened to more people. I mean, people are going to do things no one approves of whether or not they have the spells in the library. So, when it is my library, I am going to bring parts of it into the world so it will be more accessible. More witches will be able to study there when they are trying to craft thesis for their magical studies."

She carries on, babbling about her plans. All I can think about is getting Jasmine in my hands. Forcing her to bite me and gaining immortality along with her. I catch a flicker of something in the rearview, but when I look back I don't see anything.

Bind her to you.

I look around again, I swear I heard a whisper. Which is impossible considering the way Lacey is chattering. It must be my soul whispering its desires to me. Binding Jasmine to me, the very idea excites me. I feel the stirrings of desire in my cock and reach down to shift things so Lacey won't notice and think she had anything to do with it.

She will be yours, to do with as you please.

I have to squeeze my thighs together to keep my stiffening cock from rising and becoming noticeable. Maybe what I know of the spell will help distract me? I found it in Persephone's book. She wrote it originally to keep her mother from finding out about her affair with Hades. It subsumes the will of a person or persons to the caster of the spell. This isn't helping, and squeezing my cock between my thighs just feels delicious. Spells. The other spell.

Yes, power. You would be powerful beyond your wildest dreams.

With the other spell I will strip her of all her power. Perhaps I will take Lacey's power as well. And then feed her to Jasmine. Maybe we will share her. I can just see the two of us, feasting on her blood... Uuunnnhh. Not helping.

Yes. The power. The destruction. You could take over the world.

The idea of taking over the world is too much and my cock spasms, squirting its sticky fluid down the leg of my pants. Damn it. A quick spell whispered, Lacey never even noticed and the mess is gone. Removed to be left in the road left behind me.

❧

Jasmine

. . .

The guys had Leonidas's truck parked a few miles from where they found me, on the edge of the territory of the wolves I killed. All the wolves ride in the back of the truck, when I asked about it Leonidas said that their clothing was at my house.

He pulls into the driveway and I get out before he can come to my door. The house looks so desolate. I cross to the porch and put my hand on the spot next to the door. The one that I needed to touch when I first accepted the house. It almost seems to warm under my hand and tears prick my eyelids. Opening the door I go straight to Scarlett's bedroom. It is empty. Barren. Not even her scent remains behind. Sebastian's room next. He was never there much but he had a room any way. For if he wanted or needed it. It is just as devoid of his presence.

The shards of my heart crumble into smaller pieces. My bedroom is a quiet refuge as Leonidas and the wolves come in. I can hear the rhythm of their conversation, it is soothing. A vehicle pulls away but still Leonidas and Banner are talking in the kitchen.

The shadows in my room seem warm, comforting somehow. I remember the tiny creature that has a shoe fetish, a tiny burst of magic and another tea set, with hot water and all the requirements for a lovely tea time, appear in the closet. Hopefully it will please the creature. I hear the vehicle come back to my house, though I don't concern myself with it. They'll go away or someone will let them in. Not long after that I begin to smell something cooking. It smells divine. I had forgotten how good food smells when it cooks. Especially this, I think it is steak. My mouth is watering and for the first time in ages, my stomach is rumbling. Try as I might to ignore the mouthwatering scents, my stomach is not having it.

When I can take it no more I get out of the bed. Crossing my room to open the door I can hear Banner talking, "Wolves have to eat. She may forget it sometimes right now but she is part wolf. Nothing helps even a broken-hearted wolf to cheer up like good food, good company," the others in there cheer aye at that, "and good booze. The smell will draw her in and then we can cheer her. Trust me, it will work."

By the time he finishes speaking I am at the door to the kitchen and Leonidas spots me, "Sonofabitch. Banner, you called it." He hold his arms open as an invitation. The contact is an invitation I cannot resist and I walk over to him. He pulls me into his lap and gives me a squeeze as everyone else in the kitchen hollers and whoops in celebration. As he finishes his shout Banner turns back to the stove and flips a steak. I watch as he grabs a plate and begins to fill it. The conversation flows around me as I watch.

The plate filled with other things Banner grabs the steak, adding it to the plate. He grabs a fork and knife then walks over to me and presents it all with a flourish, "For you sweet Jasmine."

My eyes sting as I smile and accept the plate. "Thank you, it smells delicious." My stomach feels ready to rip itself out of my body and take over the filling of it. I don't know what to taste first. There is the steak, but also mashed potatoes and greens. The greens appear to have been cooked with bacon grease and I really want some of that just for the memories it brings to mind. I decide to go with the steak first because I figure the wolf side of me is likely to be more carnivore than herbivore. I cut into the steak, it is rare and seared just right. The first bite is heaven. I want to keep chewing for the flavor but I do swallow, so I can have more. Because I want to taste the rest as well, I dip the steak into the potatoes. So good. I try the greens next, they do not disappoint. Seasoned and cooked in bacon fat, I could eat a pound or so, it is so good. As the food on my plate starts to disappear I tune in to the conversation around me. Leonidas has a hand on my back, rubbing it occasionally. The wolves are talking about a game they played recently. I think it was supposed to be a tag football sort of game, but it sounds like tackle.

"Wait, is it tag or tackle," I ask, because I can't tell.

They all laugh and Mario answers, "It is tag football, we simply are bad at following the rules. We keep it tag so that things stay light and nobody breaks anything. Well, so no one gets too broken."

I laugh, "Was it always this way?"

Denton chimes in this time, "No. We went this route because too many people were asking questions when they would see us injured one week and back out the next. They were accusing us of witchcraft and miracles. Some of them wanted to burn us and others wanted to start a religion around us. It was bad all over. So, we quit playing for a few years and moved away from that area. When we did start playing again we kept it at tag football and we play in a remote spot. The pack got together and bought a chunk of land way out, we play roughly in the middle of it. It keeps our games private and the torches put away."

Eric laughs, "They definitely did not want to worship us the way I would prefer."

Eric is booed good-naturedly, and Banner sets a drink in front of me. He nudges it my way and says, "Try it."

It has a lovely amber color to it and it smells sweet like honey. I bring the glass to my lips and sip, the taste of honey and roses and apples explodes in my mouth. I roll it around to savor it with my eyes closed, "Mmm, Banner, this is amazing. What is it?" I open my eyes to find everyone watching me. My cheeks heat, I think I might be blushing?

Throats clear and Banner says, "It is a mead made by some of the people in our pack. Speaking of packs, I know you have had a rough time lately and don't really need another thing to think about but, this isn't going to keep for very long." The other wolves nod knowingly and I am just confused until Banner continues, "You are a beautiful woman and now a very powerful creature who is at least part shifter. Women are very valued in our culture, and also kind of scarce. Not because we don't have girls or anything, but because our birth rates are low and women are not as often added by bite as men. We believe in choice and not a lot of women want to become wolves. Not all packs believe in choice. Very soon you need to choose a pack to be part of. My pack is always open to you should you choose, but here," he passes a folded paper to me, "are two other very good packs you could be part of if you would like. I can vouch for them, they are good people."

Dario makes a face, "You should tell her all of it."

Banner narrows his eyes at Dario, "I told her everything she needs to know. Both of the packs I suggested are good. I will not unduly influence her."

Dario's face twists as he scoffs, "Bull. You are letting your own bias against your standing in the overall—"

Banner cuts him off with a snarl, "Shut up!"

"Too late Banner." I shake my head, "It was too late

when you said you had told me everything I need to know because I know that means you left shit out. Come off it."

He shakes his head, an obstinate set to his mouth, "I don't want to influence you toward my pack with something like social status. It's not right."

I sigh. Men. "I would have chosen your pack either way. I'm still not going to do anything you say. But if I need to be affiliated with a pack it will be yours as opposed to strangers. Now tell. Fucker."

Banner smiles wryly and sighs, "They wanted me to tell you that I am technically royalty and that status has an effect on my pack standing."

"Are you really going to make me drag the whole thing out of you Banner? How are you technically royalty?" Dario chuckles and I look at him, "Tell me what he is leaving out."

He smiles, "He is leaving out that he is crown prince. When his father dies or steps down, he will be the next ruler of all the wolves. Our pack has a much higher status and privileges because of it. He likes to pretend he is a regular guy, this is a regular pack. It drives his father crazy and pisses his mom off."

Banner snarls at Dario but there is no heat in it. Prince. He is a whole damn prince. I look at Banner, "When he says prince, royalty, he means of like this country, right?"

Banner looks away, "No."

"Continent?"

"Also no."

"Hemisphere?" I am grasping at straws here. He can't be...

"No. The one and only. For the world. There is only one royal family in the wolf shifter world. My family is it. Now you know." He gives me a hard look, "You better not start treating me any differently now that you know."

Leonidas, silent all this time, starts laughing. I twist to look at him and he is struggling to form words. He finally calms himself enough to say, "Of course she is going to treat you different!" Banner frowns and crosses his arms over his chest, "She is going to give you sooo much more shit. You have been hiding this princely thing because you thought she would treat you special because," he lifts his hands to make air quotes, "status. If anything she is going to work hard at making damn sure you know she is not going to be told what to do." He laughs some more, "Dumbass." His laughter is dwindling now and the others around the table are pointedly now looking at Banner.

I however, am offended as fuck, "You really thought you would get like, preferential treatment or something if I knew? You thought it would make a single fucking bit of difference to me that you are royalty?"

Banner's eyes have gotten wide and he straightens in his chair, arms no longer crossed in front of him, "Well, I , um..."

"You didn't fucking think that shit through is what you did. I will take your invitation to be a part of your pack. You can absolutely fucking count on me not ever taking a knee to you or treating you like anything other than mother-fucking Banner. Fuck around and find out sir. You try any bossy royalty bullshit on me and I will feed your balls to you. And don't think you can take back your invitation now either. I won't be part of another pack that could think to use my connection to you either. It's your pack or none."

The other wolves are having problems maintaining composure and excuse themselves to go get some fresh air outside. Leonidas is chuckling behind me and Banner is smiling a goofy smile as he says, "Welcome to the pack Jasmine. I would expect no less from you. And just so you know, that was incredibly hot. Do it again."

I laugh, "What? Sir, I was telling you off. Not seducing you."

He leans forward, "I know, that's what made it so hot."

"You are incorrigible."

He smirks, "I know. Want to teach me a lesson?"

Leonidas stays with me after everyone else leaves to go to work. I think it was by design. They all decided to leave a guardian with me to ensure I don't run away again, or at least they would be able to monitor and start searching or something? I don't know. It doesn't matter.

I could ignore the shards of my heart with everyone here. With only Leonidas, I just want to curl up and cry on his shoulder. I don't know how if he would go for that so I opt for going back to bed. He follows me to my bedroom, "Can I lay down with you?"

"If you want. I might cry on you if you do though. Sure you want to be around for that?"

He crosses the room so fast I don't even realize he has until his arms are wrapped around me. He whispers to me, "If crying on my shoulder is what you need, I am here for you. Don't ever think you have to hide your tears from me."

In a whisper I ask, "And when you leave me? When you can't take this creature I have become? What then?"

"I am not leaving. I told you, I would destroy this world before I let it have you. You are mine, it doesn't matter what you are, I love you. If I have to tear this world apart to keep you that is what I will do. Tears, they just make me want to start the destruction now, to take apart those that hurt you. The only reason Scarlett and Sebastian are still alive is because they ran away before I lost your trail. And I should probably confess that I did tell them if they were here when I returned I would remove their heads from their shoulders and put them where they belonged." He leans back to look at me, "Are you very mad?"

I can't help it, I giggle. "Where exactly were you planning to put their heads?" As much as I love them, this new part of me, the one so done with all the pain, kind of likes the idea. That scares me a little but I can't think about that right now.

A chuckle rumbles deep in his chest, "I had ideas about literally putting them where they figuratively seem to be."

Wrapping my arms around him I pull him closer, "That is possibly one of the sweetest things I have heard. I hope you really do stay with me."

His hand comes up to my chin and gently he pushes me to look up at him, "I don't give a damn if you become part Komodo Dragon, you are stuck with me. I am yours even if you send me away. When it all fucking ends, I will be there with you." His lips are so close to mine as he says that, I close the distance. My lips touch his and his arm tightens around me, lifting me as he takes control. The kiss is burning desire and fierce need.

My legs wrap around him pressing his hard cock against my throbbing core. He stumbles to the bed, never taking his lips from mine. He bumps the edge of the bed and drags his lips away, pushing me down on the bed. His gaze roams my body and he asks, "Do you want to take those off or can I get rid of them the fast way?"

I laugh, "Let's try the fast way."

No sooner does it leave my lips than he leans down and grabs the bottom edge of my shirt, ripping it down the middle. My back arches, his hands come back to my body, one tweaking a nipple while the other grabs the button for my jeans and pops it off. Through a haze of pleasure I hear it hit the floor. His hand leaves my nipple as he bends down and grabs the bottom of my jeans, snatching them off and letting them sail across the room to hit the window. He growls as he drops to his knees and pushes mine wide. His breath on my pussy makes me quiver with expectation. His tongue leaves a trail of fire from my core to my clit where he stops to flick his tongue. I press myself at his mouth and he grabs my hips, taking his talented tongue from my clit and making me cry out, "No!"

He chuckles, "You'll cum when I let you. Now hold still before I tie you down."

"Don't tempt me with a good time."

His mouth returns to my aching clit and he swirls his togue around it over and over. The pleasure builds, my hips rocking of their own accord. A finger slides into my dripping pussy, then two. The walls of my pussy start to pulse around his fingers as his pumps them in and out of me. His tongue switches to flicking back and forth across my clit and I am soaring, my body convulses with the orgasm and he stills, waiting for me to come back. As soon as I am still he withdraws his fingers and stands, licking them. "Goddamn you taste amazing."

I chuckle, "I try."

He sheds his clothing and I feel his hard cock stroking my pussy lips, and I want it inside me now. I lift my jelly legs and pull them up to give him access, he lines himself up and presses in ever so slightly before tugging at my legs to rest on his shoulders. One arm holding a leg in place the other slides down a leg to rest on my vulva, his thumb slipping between my lips to press my clit. I moan and rock my hips as he presses into me with his cock. The delicious stretching, filling feeling has me holding so still as I savor it. His hips stop touching my ass and he pauses there for a breath as we both enjoy the feeling of his cock in me.

I roll my hips slowly, just once. He growls and pulling back till just the head is left in me, he starts fucking me hard and fast. His thumb starts rubbing my clit at the same pace and I am racing toward a second orgasm with a speed I forget is possible. He picks up the pace and I know he is close too. My orgasm hits with an explosion and I am cresting as he comes, slamming into me one more time and staying buried deep in me as he fills me in a different way.

He leans down to rest his torso on mine, our bodies still connected and too sensitive to move.

Eighteen

Jasmine

I am getting ready to head to one of my magic lessons when my phone rings. A cold lump forms in the pit of my stomach but I answer.

It's Jan on the phone, "Hi Jasmine, I need to cancel today. Um, actually, we need to cancel the next few weeks while we deal with things here."

"Oh no, I hope everything is ok?" I ask, hoping against hope this isn't because of what I am.

"Well, a witch was murdered. We know it was another witch that did it, but we can't figure out who and it was pretty awful so we want to focus on this."

I gasp, "I am so sorry. I completely understand. You say it is a witch you all can't identify? As in someone that has been keeping their identity secret, someone relatively new to the area?"

"Yes, why? Jasmine, do you know something about this?"

I bite my lip. I am probably not getting another lesson in magic again. But at least they will be safe. "I think it might be connected with some things that have been happening in my corner of the world. There was a witch working with Mikael when I fought him to his death. The witch is still around and he recently killed a wolf friend of ours."

Jan is silent for a long time before she sighs and says, "So this may be that same witch trying to get at you."

I nod but remember she can't see that. Clearing the lump that has suddenly appeared in my throat I say, "It is probably that they are the same people, yes."

"We are going to need to discuss this among ourselves. We will call you and let you know once we decide whether it will be safe for us to continue your lessons."

"I understand. I am so sorry that any of this touched your lives. Please accept my condolences. If you don't mind, let me know where I can send a gift to the deceased's family."

"She doesn't actually have any family. We were going to pool our resources to pay for her funeral expenses."

"If you will let me, I will pay for them. It is the least I could do. Please say you will let me pay those."

"Really? You would?"

I can hear the disbelief in her voice. It only makes me more determined. "Yes. I will. Have the funeral home call me, I will give them permissions and sign whatever they need. Or get it all planned and I will just pay for it. Whatever you all want, I am not worried about the cost."

I can hear her crying as she says, "I will. Thank you. Thank you so much. You don't—"

"I do understand. Until recently, I was raggedy assed trailer park poor. I came into an inheritance and now, well, I don't have to worry about it. This will allow me to repay you all in some small way for the time spent helping me."

"You are so appreciated. And I want you to know, however the decision goes, it isn't that we are concerned for what you have become."

"What? You know about that?"

"Oh, yes. Sally overheard a couple of vampires talking about it, saying it was un-natural and blah, blah. Sally laughed because they say that about us too. She told us about it, so that we could have better reactions. We didn't want our surprise to possibly make you feel like we wouldn't accept that. No, if we discontinue lessons it will be for our own safety and nothing else. I don't know that we will, but I have to at least make sure everyone is informed. You understand, don't you?"

"I do, and I want you all safe. That is why I was up front with you. I never thought that this would affect you all. The vampires, did Sally happen to mention what they looked like?"

Jan sighs, "I had hoped you wouldn't ask that. She recognized them. It was Scarlett and Sebastian."

"I see." I swallow as my heart breaks anew, "Thank you for telling me. I-I need to go, I have some things I need to attend to now. I wish you all safe and happy lives. Thank you." I hit the end button before she can say anything. The ache in my heart is turning into a fire and I want to rage at something, someone, anything. A scream rips from my throat as my body shifts to wolf. I don't want to stay here right now so I hit the door with magic so it opens and closes behind me. Once outside I stand still for a moment, feeling the moonlight on my fur. Some nosy cunt gasps when she sees me and starts screaming for her husband to get the gun. I lift a lip and growl at her before I bound into the wooded area. As I run I hear two shots fired into the wooded area and I nearly turn around to rip their throats out. As I start though, Hekate's image appears in front of me and she kneels in front of me. I hear her voice in the wind, "Don't shit where you live little one."

Solid advice and I heed it, running away. Running from the fire of vengeance that is burning in my heart now.

Hake

Killing that witch felt good. I look over at Lacey, laying things out for the spell I plan and not a hint of concern. I make my own preparations. It is finally happening. Tonight, tonight I will have control over Jasmine. She will be mine to do with as I please. My cock grows hard at the very thought of the things I will be able to have her do.

Lacey clears her throat loudly, dragging me away from pleasant thoughts, "Hake, I am finished. Everything is ready. Are you ok?"

I put on my most comforting smile, "I was simply lost in daydreams. Every thing is laid out precisely as I instructed?"

She rolls her eyes, "I'm not new you know." She prattles on, reciting to me exactly how she laid everything out as I palm the ritual knife and thank all my lucky stars that I memorized the spell for stealing a witches power. Lacey's back is to me, there will not be another moment more perfect. Stepping closer to her I stab her in the side of her neck, hopefully catching a main artery before I snatch the knife back out with a twist. She cries out and spins to look at me, "Why?"

I smile that same comforting smile as I begin the spell to steal her power before she dies. Her blood is pouring out so fast, I barely get the spell done as she seems to stop breathing. I feel the power rushing into my body and it is amazing. I feel like I could stop time. I want this to never end, I need to get Jasmine under my control now. With controlled movement I work through the spell. It goes out, traveling over land, racing to her. It hits her, claws sinking in. I command her, "Come to me now!" She fights the compulsion, it almost feels like she is trying to throw the spell off. I amp up the compulsion, commanding her again, "Come to me! You are mine! Come to your master. Bend your will to mine, I have you already. Fighting will only hurt you. Now come to me!"

The very next thing I feel is a blast of power slamming into me through the connection, throwing me across the room. I hit the wall and darkness claims me as I crumple to the floor.

Jasmine

When I get back to the house there are a couple wolves there waiting. It is Dario and Denton, they tell me that they were sent to be my company. I laugh, "That's great. How about we hang on the porch and have drinks while we wait for Leonidas and Banner to arrive. I assume it was them that sent you?"

They tell me it was, and the fire in me banks itself a little more with the pleasure I feel at their concern. We get our drinks and they remind me that I need food too. It is amazing how quickly I adjusted to not worrying about food at all. I order a stack of pizzas, knowing that they will get eaten.

We are sitting on the front porch eating pizza and sipping our drinks as I tell them the story of how I met Leonidas. I am just at the part where I tell him fuck you when this agonizing pain rips through my belly and I scream as I grab at my belly, dropping drink and pizza.

Dario is at my side in an instant, "What's wrong? What's happening?"

I grit my teeth through the pain and tell him, "Someone is trying to take my will. Aaaaaagggh!" The pain is so intense. I can hear Denton talking to someone as Dario sits with me through the pain. The one trying to take my will, he commands me to him and when I don't do what he says the pain worsens. "Ah, Hekate, I don't know if I can take this pain!"

He is commanding me again, Dario is telling Denton to grab the chains out of the truck. Hekate's ghostly form appears in front of me, "I can't physically help you." I sob in fear that I will have to go to this person, "But I can offer information. If he is unconscious the compulsion won't be so powerful and the connection between you goes both ways."

Dario flinches away from my smile, and I close my eyes, accessing the power inside me. I send the biggest blast I can with the pain distracting me through the connection between us. The compulsion drops to a manageable level and I sigh in relief. "Thank you Hekate. Your knowledge is greatly appreciated."

I hear Denton telling Banner everything that he could see happening, including how I glowed when I sent that bolt of power to the asshole that did this.

Nineteen

Jasmine

I see the chains when they bring them up to the porch and I tell them, "If you try to put those chains on me, I'm going to bite you in a way you won't like."

Denton says, "We are just trying to help you. If you don't want them, we won't use them."

The compulsion to go to him is still there and it hurts. Not so much as when he was awake but fuck me, it hurts enough. Leonidas skids to a stop in front of the house, he and Banner are before me in an instant. "Has anyone called Demetris? Nia? Anyone that might know more than we do?"

Dario shrugs, "I don't even know who they are? And I don't know any witches."

Leonidas looks back at me, "Jasmine, where is your phone?"

I point at the table with the pizza boxes, he snatches it up and holds it up to my face to unlock, then flips through to find the number still labeled Father Neally. "Demetris, she needs you right now. Something has her, it is trying to force her to them and it is hurting her to resist."

"Oh no! Bring her to the library, I will open the door."

Leonidas hits end just as the guy trying to force me to him wakes up, the pain doubles and I want to run to the fucker so I can pull his spine out from the front. "Fuck me it hurts so damn bad," I grit out as I break the arms of the chair squeezing them with the pain.

"Can you walk?" Leonidas asks and I don't have the energy to fight for walking so I shake my head no. "I'm going to pick you up and carry you. Is that ok?"

"Yes. Bring. Bring. The. Chains."

Leonidas nods and scoops me up, everyone following behind us. The door to the library is standing open and Demetris holding it, telling Leonidas to hurry. We get into the library and I tell them, "You better chain me up, I don't know how much longer I can resist."

They wrap me up in chains as Demetris and Nia study me. I see the looks they exchange and I know its bad. Demetris kneels before me, "Jasmine, the hooks are double barbed. We can't remove them, and they are growing besides that."

I grit out, "Can't we just cut them? So he isn't attached anymore?" Sweat is trickling down my body, such an odd feeling in comparison to the pain.

Demetris shakes his head no, "If we cut them the rebound would most likely kill you."

"Are you sure? I say we cut the fucking lines, rebound be damned. Call it science."

A man's image appears in the library, he looks me over and laughs, I want to kill him slowly. Wait, I know him. He is that guy, Hake, that I met at the book store. The guy that was trying to stalk me. Oh gods, this is all my fault. He says, "Release her to come to me like the good little bitch she is."

Leonidas is at the image and rips through it before he is done speaking. The man laughs again, "Stupid vampire. This is only a projection. Release her to come to me or I will start playing with some of the other, more interesting spells in the books I acquired from this illustrious library."

Demetris asks, "Why do you want her?"

Hake sneers, his face twisted in such a way it is ugly, "Because she is mine." Leonidas and Banner both growl at that, the man laughs, "Stupid. What will you do? Nothing, absolutely nothing. Because anything you do will get her killed."

Demetris says, "Why don't we meet somewhere neutral, just you, me, and her."

Hake scowls at that, "No. Release her now. If she is not with me in the next half hour, I will finish the spell that will destroy this state and most of its inhabitants."

Tears roll down my face, I know what has to happen. I can't let so many innocent people die for me. The memory of Helen's death wracks me with guilt, too many have died for me already. I look around the room at the conversation buzzing around me, all these people that I love ready to die for me. I can't let that happen.

Twenty

Jasmine

None of them are watching me and I pull magic, ready to do what I must. Nia looks at me, she must feel the magic. I freeze, till she very deliberately closes her eyes and inclines her head just a fraction of an inch. I know she realizes what conclusion I have come to and supports me in this and I appreciate her so much. Using my magic I make multiple links on both sides of the chains holding me disappear. Using every bit of speed I can muster I run out of the library, long before the chains hit the floor. Outside I turn for Mikael's old place. I know that is where this Hake is, I can feel it. As I run Hekate's image appears ahead of me but to the right, and she is keeping pace with me.

I tell her, "I have to save them. I have to go."

Hekate nods, "I know. It can be no other way. You need to know, you have the power to stop this. It will be easier to think once you are where he wants you, the pain clouding your mind will be gone. Also, I cannot help you right now. This is part of the warring occurrences, I am bound by the rules of it unless Cronos acts. I am watching, I will be with you the entire time my darling daughter of my heart. I know you can do this."

She disappears as I arrive at the house. It is well lit and seems from the outside as if nothing ever happened. I stop to look at it and on closer inspection I can see the magic covering things. So it is still a wreck, good. I can use that.

I step into the house and I see him waiting for me. He is nothing special. I can see Lacey's spirit hanging around him. So she is dead too. One more death to lay at my door. The pain drops away like it never was. He smiles at me and my stomach turns, how did I ever think him even the least bit attractive?

I stand in the doorway as he sips his drink, it smells like a screwdriver. The kind they made with the cheapest vodka they could find to give away free at the dive bars when I was younger. He sets his drink down and says, "Good girl. You should get to love hearing me say that, because if you aren't a good girl I will make every fiber of your being writhe in agony. I know you will be my good girl now that you have a reason to behave. For now, come here. Let's get to know each other better." He drones on and on as I step into the house fully. I leave the door open because fuck him. He is going on about how he will have me turn him and what a perfect team we will make but all I can see are the scorch marks where Mikael died. A ghost of an idea sparks within me and I close my eyes to see my spiritual body, all the magical bits that this fucker put barbed wire through. The barbs are a muddy black color, angry and biting. As I study them I realize they only look like a strong metal wire. I move further in, seeking my inner flame the way Helen taught me. I see the barbs surrounding it, but they burn and crumble to dust if they get too close.

I feel certain that my idea will work and I start to— my head rocks back with the slap from Hake and my eyes fly open. "You'll fucking well pay attention when I speak to you!" Pain lances through me and I double over. He grabs my arm and hauls me up to face him, shoving scraps of lace into my hands, "You get your ass into this now."

I suck in a breath and grate out, "Fuck you." He smiles and turns on the compulsion, making the pain a hundred times worse and my legs give out, sending me crashing to the floor.

Twenty-One

Leonidas

We are still trying to decide what to do when I hear the chains hit the floor. I know immediately that she is gone but I spin around like I could catch her anyway. I knew, I knew she wouldn't let us risk our lives for her. I never should have let myself be distracted. She must have been waiting for her chance. She probably believes it better this way since those two cowards left her. This situation and her being freshly abandoned is exactly what Hekate warned against! I shove a hand through my hair and Demetris asks, "Do we know where she is going?"

My eyes meet Banner's and we both say, "Mikael's place."

Demetris sighs, "The place the door opened into. The one that she had such a strong reaction to seeing the scorch marks in."

I nod, "That's the one. We should get going. Who knows what this sick bastard will try to do and fast as she is... She is probably halfway there while we are still fucking about." I head for the door because I am leaving now, whether or not anyone else comes along. I am unsurprised when Banner falls in next to me, "Think you can keep up prince?"

"Fuck off. I may have to bite you when all this is done."

"Promises, promises." We step out into the night air and I realize Nia and Demetris are right behind us, "You two can keep up, right?"

Nia glares at me and I shrug before I take off. Jasmine's trail is a little easier to follow now that she is wolf, it made her scent easier to detect because she actually sweats again. It's an odd thing, a vampire having a pulse and warmth. Not that vampires in general don't have heart beat or pulses of a sort, just that they are very slowed in comparison to most other creatures. Slow enough that they aren't usually detected. The scent of her gets stronger as we follow and then a scent of something else is with her. I don't recognize the scent exactly but it smells...powerful?

We get to the house and coming up the driveway I can see the door standing open, my little rebel, always with the fuck you's. He is yelling at her and then she falls to the ground, thrashing in pain. The man grabs at her clothing as I get close, I put on a burst of speed fueled by rage. How dare this piece of trash try to— I barrel into him and we fly across the room, landing hard on the floor. The breath is knocked out of the asshole and I raise up, keeping a grip on him till something blasts me off him, even as my fingers dig into his flesh, I still hit the wall and bounce off to land on my feet. Demetris and Nia are trying to help Jasmine and I want to go to her but I start back for him anyway. Banner hits the bastard in wolf form, biting his arm and ripping it half off.

Demetris and Nia are running away from Jasmine screaming, "Take cover!" Jasmine is on fire, her eyes open and unseeing. Shit, the last time I saw her like that she leveled a fucking house. I run for a table and pull it over onto its side as I jump over it. I just hope Banner managed to find cover as flames explode through the room.

Twenty-Two

Jasmine

Hake's screams are music to my ears. The pain is gone and so is whatever bound me to him. He is going to pay for what he did and for what he planned. I walk toward him, he is bloody and burnt, but starts yelling at me, "Jasmine! You pick me up and get me out of here! Defend me! Kill the ones that did this to me!"

His voice becomes more shrill with each word as the realization that I am no longer bound to him dawns. I laugh at the terror in his eyes and keep stalking over to him as he scrambles to put a hand in his pocket. He pulls out what looks like a glass ball and smashes it on himself, disappearing from sight. I run over to make certain he isn't just invisible but he is gone. I scream in frustration, "Fuck! I should have stopped him!" I want to lash out at something, anything, but I hear a whimper and the red recedes from my vision. I look behind me and there is Banner, struggling to stand. One of his paws isn't sitting quite right, oh no. Is this because of me? I run to him, lifting his singed body and taking the weight from his injured paw.

Because I know he loves a good joke I ask, "Is there a vet nearby that we can take him to?" He growls at me and I chuckle, "Come on, that was funny."

Demetris stands from behind a couch and Nia rises with him. He says, "I can set his paw so he can heal and then shift. His healing should go quickly once the bones are sitting in the right place."

Nia walks around the couch, "I can ease the pain of the setting and the superficial wounds."

I know she means the burns but is trying not to make me feel guilty about it. I can see the burns on them, though they are healing. And Leonidas, he has soot on himself. I don't know whether it is from landing in old stuff or if it is new and he is healed already. I have hurt my friends once again, this time myself. Maybe... Maybe it isn't safe for me to be around anyone? Leonidas flips a table back on its legs and says, "Lay his big ass here."

I smile and walk over to lay Banner on the table as gently as possible. Demetris is standing next to me as I lay him down and helps to ease the transition. Nia is on the other side of the table when I look up, she smiles softly at me. My eyes blur with unshed tears when I see the sooty smudge on her face, though it is already healed. Blinking fast I start to move away from the table but a paw grabs me, claws digging into my arm. Banner whimpers and Leonidas is behind me, arms wrapping around me, begging with his body for me to stay near. I acquiesce because in truth, I don't want to leave them either. My eyes eventually clear and I see Banner watching me with the one eye facing me as Demetris sets his paw. I reach out and bury my hands in the thick fur on his side and he sighs. Leonidas chuckles, his chest vibrating with it against my back.

Once we got Banner's paw set he healed quickly and was able to shift to his human form. Now, we need to find those books, if they are still here. "Let's go over the house. Hopefully he left them here in his haste to get away from me."

We all split up and I head for the stairs. I know he used that one room before, perhaps he went back? Going in the room again is eerie. It wasn't magically reinforced like the front rooms. The hole in the wall is there, but no magical items or ritual space set up. I am glad that I mostly don't use those things. Seems pretty and probably fun but also a giant pain.

Stepping out of the room I look down the hall in time to see Banner poke his head out of a room, "Hey, c'mere."

I walk down the hall and stop at the door he peeped out of, holy shit. The walls are lined with old books. I am stunned and horrified. How are we going to find out if they are here in time to stop him if they aren't? I step into the room and stop next to Banner, "Holy shit. How are we going to find them in all this?"

"Maybe they haven't touched all of them?"

I nod, "I'll start on the left, you check the right." On the left wall is a ladder, it's mate over at the right wall. I check the lower books. So far, all I smell is Mikael. That could be good. Maybe the books will be hidden in here and Hake is just depending on us to be to dumb to check all the books. Would he even think about us sniffing them out? Up the ladder, the books near the top have been here a long time.

Even the smell of Mikael is fading from them. I use the rail to move my ladder over to the next section, nothing so far. Four more sections of the same, with a pause to explain what we were doing to everyone else as they came in. Leonidas started working with me, he taking the lower shelves and tugging my ladder along with him. Nia took the back wall with Demetris working with her toward Banner.

Suddenly I pick up a different scent, "Leonidas, move the ladder over a little more. I smell something different but I can't quite reach it." He stops sniffing books and slides the ladder over, watching me for a sign to stop. I get close to the smell and I hold my hand out toward him palm out. He stops and I lean in toward the scent. It is Hake's. Reaching in I grab the books and I feel the spell activate as I pull them back, "Spell!" I scream as I am blown off the ladder. The floor rushes up and I land hard. The ceiling is really very pretty from here. Nice scrollwork on the moulding. There is an incredibly loud ringing noise that just won't stop and everything on my body feels weighted. Slowly the ringing fades and I hear Nia whispering. "Speak up Nia, I can't quite catch what you're saying."

Leonidas and Banner both lean over me, "Sh, just lay there and relax. It will all be better soon."

"You guys are cute when you work together," I tell them with what I hope is a sexy smile. Leonidas chuckles and Banner rolls his eyes, saying, "Now she wants me. Of course. Spell addled and that is when she wants me."

Leonidas scowls, "Not just you. She wants me too."

Banner scowls right back, "And that's nothing new. The wanting me is and that is what I am focusing on."

The heaviness that seemed to be weighing me down lifts

and I can hear Nia telling them, "It's done. She may be a little off from the fall but the spell is gone now."

Lifting my head to look at her, "Was anyone else hurt?"

She growls at me, "No! Impetuous idiot!What were you thinking grabbing the books like that?"

I look down at my hand still clutching the books and hold them up with a grin, "I'm an impetuous idiot with the books. Maybe that counts for something?"

Her eyes roll and she storms off as Demetris kneel near my hand, "Can you set the books down on the floor here. I would like to examine them before anymore touching of the books happens."

Setting the books carefully on the floor I let go and sit up. My hand itches and I look at it, it is healing. It looks like it was massively burned by holding onto the books. Perfect. Within a minute it is healed like there was never anything there.

Demetris is studying the books hard without touching them so I look at them with the other sight. It is like a spider web was laid on each book individually and another on the three of them. I see the string to unravel the outer spell and I don't think Demetris has yet. "The string to unravel it is right here," I tell him, pointing at the strand.

He looks up at me, "What do you mean string?"

"Is that wrong?"

He shrugs, "No, but it isn't how I see it. What do you see?"

"Oh! I see webs. One around each book and another around the three of the books as a whole."

He rubs his chin, "And the string you see, what would that unravel?"

"Just the outer one as far as I can tell."

He looks at Leonidas and Banner, "You two back away." He casts a set of three shields, one around the books and one around each of us, "Pull the string now."

He is watching intently so I go slowly, he obviously wants to know how this works for me. Grabbing the tiny bit sticking out I start pulling and the cord unwraps from the stack of books. When I have pulled the whole thing away from the books the crossing lines melt away and so does the string I pulled. I look up at Demetris when he grunts, "It's gone. Can you find the string on the top book?"

I repeat the process with each of the books and Demetris watches hard the whole time. When I finish the last book he drops the shields and tells me to pick the top book up. Extending my hand I let it hover over the book for a moment, I really don't want to get blasted across the room again and what if I was wrong? Deep breath and I pick up the book, scrunching my eyes closed in preparation for... nothing. Nothing happens. "It worked!"

Demetris chuckles, "It did. And now, how did you learn that? To see it that way?"

"Um, Hekate spent a lot of time training me. Like, we did in person meets but she came to me in my dreams a lot. While we were there she taught me how to see things a little different. She said I used to know this, but even restored memories lose things. Small things fade away leaving the bigger. So she was showing me the things I learned in another life I guess. Or maybe just helping me to remember them? I'm not sure. Either way, when I choose to see the magic, to look at a spell, it usually looks like a web of some sort. Why? Is that weird or something?"

His eyes have gotten more round as I spoke and I am kind of concerned that he regrets letting Alena make me librarian. He is shaking his head in what looks like disbelief, "That method hasn't been taught in so long that it was a myth, a legend in my time."

Shrugging I tell him, "Hekate was probably around before you too. You can take it up with her if you want."

His eyes bug out and focus on something behind me. I turn and Hekate is standing behind me, "Oh hi!"

She looks down at me, "You know better than to grab magic books without checking them first."

Casting my eyes down I say, "I do. I got excited and didn't think. It won't happen again."

"Get up dear one, I won't be yelling at you. I think the spell that hit you did quite enough. My yelling would do nothing productive." I get up and she hugs me, before looking to Demetris, "You should close your mouth, it is very rude to stare, more so with your mouth hanging open like that."

Demetris' mouth closes so fast I hear his teeth clack together, "I, um, hmm. My apologies."

He seems to be blushing? "Demetris, are you blushing?"

His face scrunches into a scowl and Hekate says, "I don't think he wants you to point that out dear. Now," she gestures round the room, "all of this must go into the library. We cannot leave it all collected here and uncovered like this. It had a spell on it to keep it hidden that would have lasted for an eternity or so but, when Hake came back here he saw the magic in the room and uncovered it all. While I could set another spell to hide it," she looks at Demetris with a grin that is a little terrifying, "we already have an entire library hidden in the folds of time. Libraries are where books belong, don't you think?"

Demetris swallows and his brow beads with sweat, "Yes.

That is exactly where books belong. I will make sure they all go in myself. Is there anything else you require, Queen?"

One of her perfect brows arches up at the honorific, "No. I think we are good. For now. Go. Get to it." He near sprints away as Hekate turns to me, "You must find him. Hake cannot be allowed to walk the Earth with the knowledge he acquired from those books. It is your job to track him down and put an end to him. Do you understand?"

My jaw tightens and I nod, "I do. And putting an end to him is definitely something I want to do. He deserves it for what—" my voice cracks and I look away as my face burns.

Hekate touches my face so gently and turns it back to her, "I know. I know. And if you make him hurt a lot," one shoulder lifts and drops, "well, as long as the end goal is accomplished it makes no difference. I love you little fighter. Go forth and destroy."

She fades away into nothing, leaving me staring at the books across the room. I blink and realize I have been staring at those books for some time. The other side of the room is nearly empty. I rush over to help.

Twenty-Three

JASMINE

I wonder how many of the books we have moved tonight have a duplicate in the library? Oh fuck, what if there are no duplicates? I am going to spend the next three lifetimes or so just trying to read it all. I mean, not the worst way to pass the time...

"Jasmine, earth to Jasmine."

I look around and realize people are talking to me, and I have been buried so deep in my thoughts that I never heard them, "Yes, sorry. I was thinking."

Demetris chuckles, "Hard thoughts to keep you that distracted. We were discussing how to find Hake. You have to eliminate him and to do that we have to figure out where he is."

"Yeah. I am not sure how I am going to do that. I feel fairly certain that he will want to come after me again but waiting for an attack doesn't sit well with me. I feel like I have done to much letting others attack me lately."

Nia looks up from the book she is perusing, "You know,

there are probably bits of him all over the place right now. Under Leonidas's nails, in Banner's teeth, probably on the floor out there. Be great for a finding spell."

Her eyes are back on the book before she stops speaking, looks like a treatise on elves. I should make sure to read that one. "She has a point. Guys, let's see. Leonidas, clean your nails into this tray." I tell him as I grab a notions dish and empty it on the floor as I walk toward him. "Banner, going to need you to shift so I can check your teeth." He jumps down from the ladder with a stack of books and sets them carefully down before shifting. I call in a set of tweezers and kneel in front of him. He opens his mouth and I can smell it. That smell unique to Hake. I could be all right with never smelling that again. Studying his teeth, they are wicked looking. I find a small string of flesh between the back teeth on the right side of his lower jaw. Using the tweezers I pull it out and look around for a place to put it. Leonidas is by my side when I look to the right, holding out the dish he cleaned his nails into. I tell him, "Thank you love," as I drop it in. Back to Banner's mouth I check the uppers and find a lovely chunk wedged in between a couple teeth. I work it out as I tell him, "You must have had a hella grip on him. You've got flesh wedged in your teeth sir. Does it always get wedged in like that or is it because he struggled?"

Banner changes again as soon as my hands are out of his mouth and is slow to pick up his towel as he says, "Asking me questions while I am shifted and you have your hands in my mouth? What the hell?" I laugh as he goes on, "The answer to your question is that stuff always gets stuck in there because nothing wants to have chunks ripped off of it and they don't give a single fuck about how hungry I might be. Jeez." He gets his towel tucked in place as I dissolve in laughter. Leonidas is struggling mightily with not laughing but I think he is losing the battle. While naked Banner is mightily distracting because he has muscles for miles and a dick I would love to have buried in me, his offense at the talking while my hands were in his mouth was hilarious. Banner scowls at me, "Don't you have some more flesh to collect?"

Leonidas, still smirking, helps me up and we head for the other room. Hake's bits are kind of laying in here. Leonidas goes to the other room for the tray while I wait. I don't really want to hold a handful of Hake till he gets back. Lacey's spirit appears in front of me, she looks angry as fuck. "I'm sorry you died in all this Lacey."

She scowls harder and I hear her voice, so low I have to focus on it, "Are you going to kill him?"

"I am. He has to die."

Her smile when I say that could light the room if she wasn't only a spirit. She says, "Good. I'll be waiting for him," before she fades away to nothing.

I am still shaking my head when Leonidas returns with the tray. "Fabulous. Let's pick up the bits and get out of here."

He doesn't ask why and we get the bits of Hake picked up quickly before we head back to help with the rest of the books.

Our task with the books finished, we are all relaxing in the library, staring at the piles of books. I can see Nia doesn't actually want to put them away, and she has been really good to me. Pulling out my phone I call Caden and tell him to come to the library, I have a surprise for him. He is snarly on the phone but we quickly hear the door opening. He walks through the books in a daze. Near drooling over some of the titles. He stops near where we all are and looks at me, "I apologize for every mean thing I ever said about you. You are fantastic and I forgive you for everything." My jaw drops as he turns and picking up a few books off a stack he heads off into the library stacks to put them away.

Which is odd because where... "Demetris, what is he going to do with the books? There isn't space for them all right now."

He looks confused a moment before he says, "I forget you wouldn't know. The library expands with additions. That spell was put on it when it was first built. The Ptolemy family had it built into the building itself. They paid exorbitant amounts to make sure this library would never be too small to house their collection. For all that their obsession was not a good idea, they really did execute it very well."

"Wow. That is amazing. So he is just going to walk around putting away books and the library will just continue to open up shelf space as he needs it?"

"Essentially, yes."

Nia looks up from her book and says, "Maybe we should do the spell to find him now?"

Ten minutes later we have everything set up and Nia does the spell since she knows it and it is pretty fucking complex. I am still kind of a bash my way through type with my magic, destroying something is way easier than finding a whole person that isn't interested in being found. She gets the place pin-pointed on a magical map that Demetris pulled out of some little cubby. He said it was enchanted to show the area it was in and wasn't interested in talking about it much more than that. Makes me wonder what kind of shady things he has gotten up to, I would love to hear those stories.

The spell pinpoints the spot and Demetris makes the map zoom in till we can see the place. Google maps has nothing on this street view. He is hiding in a bar in the magic sector, not far from where Helen died. Dammit. This is the last fucking place I want to go. It is odd that he would happen to have a place to hide so close to the restaurant we went to when she was murdered. But, that has to just be a coincidence. There's no way he was there and happened to be at the restaurant right then to see us. And besides, what reason would he have to murder Helen? How would he even have known she was with me? The whole idea is ridiculous and I am not even going to entertain it. Except, what if he did see us going in the restaurant? What if he is the reason I don't have Helen as my friend and mentor? The idea hurts. It may very well be my fault again that another someone I love was hurt or died. Just for being a part of my life.

Twenty-Four

One trip to a store later we are heading for the bar he is hiding at. From what we could see he is holed up in a space above the bar. We park about a mile away from the place and walk over as if we are just wandering the area. After circling the building and wandering off I lead the way into an alley the I am pretty sure will give us a good view of the place. Sure enough, we go around a corner and there is the door to his place. I conjure in a couple chairs, no point in being uncomfortable while we wait. Three hours later I spot him walking past one of the windows. Well, I say walking but it looked like every step caused him pain and it gave me great delight. I could have watched that all day but eventually we couldn't see him from the window and when I would have gone up to peek in Leonidas stopped me. He says that magical people have a thing about peeping in windows too.

With a shrug I nod, I guess I can wait. It will definitely be better if I can take him elsewhere before I do the things I want to do to him.

Now that we have seen what we came to see I send the chairs back. I cast a spell that Nia taught me at the front door to his place and watch it spread over the entire building. Once it is done Leonidas and I wander the magical sector stores. He makes sure that we never go too close to the restaurant where Helen died and I am grateful. The sun finally sets and we climb a fire escape on a building near his place to set up one of the cameras we picked up earlier after I call them to us from the truck we left parked. The cameras are solar and we leave a small wifi so that we can have access to the recordings at any time. Now if we can just remember to check them.

Walking back down the fire escape we are a lot more leisurely. Leonidas holds my hand as we walk past the bar on our way to the truck. He spots a small garden and is pulling me toward it when we hear my name called out. I turn toward a voice I haven't heard in some time. A voice I still miss even if the last time I heard it was not the most pleasant time.

Scarlett's face is twisted in rage and Sebastian stands next to her, disgust plain on his face as he looks me over. My heart breaks all over seeing the way they both feel about me written so plain on their faces.

Scarlett sneers at me, "What are you doing here abomination? Shouldn't you be somewhere hiding what you are?"

Broken heart or not, I won't cry in front of them. "That is your opinion Scarlett. Unless you would like to take it up with Hekate?"

She laughs, "What? You need a goddess to fight your battles for you?"

Sighing, I say, "Are you planning to fight me Scarlett? Is that where you're at now? You feel a way about me and so you need to fight me?"

Scarlett plants her feet, "I'm not just going to fight you, I am going to get rid of the abomination before me."

Sebastian's eyes go wide, I don't think he knew she was planning that. He grabs her arm and jerks her toward him, whispering furiously in her ear. I wait to see if he manages to talk her down.

She scowls at him and turns back to me but he gives her arm a jerk, his teeth gritted together. She stares at him for a long moment, I can only guess at what he is saying. His face reveals nothing while hers is just angry. I hate to see her like this. I want to hug her. And slap her. She snatches her arm out of his grip and I brace myself in case she doesn't listen to him. Scarlett faces me again, her eyes roam the crowd that has begun to gather.

Leonidas gives the hand he still holds a squeeze, reminding me that I am not alone in this. Scarlett looks me up and down, her lip curls. "You're not worth the trouble." She turns and walks away.

Sebastian looks at me, his beautiful lips pressed into a thin line. His eyes soften and his lips tremble before he turns away and swiftly catches up to Scarlett. I feel a single tear rolling down my face and I dash it away, scrubbing my cheek with fingers curled into a fist. Leonidas brings my other hand to his lips and presses a soft kiss on my fingers, murmuring, "Let's go home."

I nod and we turn back toward the truck.

Twenty-Five

It is nearing morning when we get back home. Banner pulls into my driveway as the sun is coming up. I look at Leonidas with a question on my lips. He answers before I can speak it, "I have to go handle some of the major decisions out at the site. But, with all that is going on, I don't want you to be alone." He narrows his eyes at me, "In part because I can't trust that you will stay put. So I asked Banner to come here after he got done. He'll mostly just sleep on your couch but if you go somewhere, can you please just take him with you?" He runs a hand across the back of his neck, "I know people say I am a fool for trusting him with you knowing he wants you and that you want him too. I don't care about that. I know I can trust him to do everything in his power to keep you safe. That is what I care about."

"Aw, give me a hug pal. You can trust me to keep her safe for sure, even if I have to sit on her to do it," Banner says from the door as he holds his arms out for a hug.

Leonidas shakes his head with a smile and walks over, the two hug and it is the best thing I have seen all night. Leonidas comes to the oversize chair I am still sitting in and hugs me, then tips my chin up to give me a kiss that curls my toes.

"Sir, keep that up and your important business will have to wait."

He laughs and kisses my forehead, "Please, just take him with you if you leave the house. Ok?"

"I will. I promise." He nods and sighs in relief. Then he walks out of the house, closing the door gently behind him.

Banner is already on the couch, pulling a throw over himself. I tell him, "Hey, you could sleep in any of the beds here you know."

He doesn't even open his eyes to tell me, "Nope. Rather be out here where I can hear the doors better. And be there if someone knocks. Couch is nice. Better than what I have at home. Alena had good taste in a couch."

Shaking my head I get up and head for my room and the shower that is calling my name.

After my shower I decided to grab some books from the library. I left the door open so Banner wouldn't worry while I was in there. I don't think he even noticed. I pulled out two on the more basic magic stuff fund wandered off to the kitchen. One really great thing about being an abomination is that I get to eat again. Drink tea. I missed the ritual of drinking tea more than anything, it is soothing. After setting the books on the table I turned on the kettle and pulled out a tea bag along with my favorite cup. Minutes later I am sitting down with a hot cup of white peach oolong tea and opening the first book.

I finish that book and look up, my stomach is growling and I realize it has been hours. My tea is long gone, even the bag is almost dry. I can't remember the last time I sat down and read a book of any kind cover to cover. Setting the book on the table I stand and stretch. I need food. Rummaging through the freezer I find that I have a lot of stuff I didn't buy. Leonidas. He is so good to me. I've never had a man actually concern himself with whether or not I ate and maybe I am expecting the minimum at this point but, gosh its nice to find that he put food in here just for me.

I grab a couple chops out, I figure Banner will be hungry eventually when he wakes up. Stopping as I am stepping away from the freezer I look at the two chops in my hand. That is not going to be enough. I seem to burn through food at a rate that is incredible now, considering I also drink blood. I grab three more chops out and let the door swing shut. Pulling out a huge cast iron pan I put some oil in and turn on the burner. While that heats I grab some noodles and a pot. Filling it with water and setting it on another burner, I salt it and turn on that burner.

It doesn't take long for the chops to fill the room with that amazing scent. The noodles are done so I pull out the colander to drain them. After they are drained I dump them in a bowl with butter, salt, garlic, oregano, and parmesan. The chops are nearly done when Banner walks in saying, "Please tell me you made enough for me to have some."

I laugh, "Yes I did. Grab plates, these chops are done." He pulls plates out and holds them out toward me, one in each hand. I load them up with chops and then with the noodles. Grabbings forks and knives I take the plate with two chops from him and hand over a set of utensils. We sit down to eat at the table and silence reigns supreme at first. The chops are so good and the noodles make my mouth want to dance in joy. As the hole starts to feel less empty I ask Banner, "Sleep well?"

He raises a brow at me, "Could have slept better if you had curled up with me. Good thing I recognize the scent of the library too, or that would have had me up and checking on you."

"You heard the door?"

"No, I smelled the library and the new scent woke me. But once I was able to place it I felt relatively certain you weren't trying to sneak off so I relaxed. And was rewarded when you came back with the books and made tea. That tea smelled amazing."

"I could make you some, if you would like?"

"Yes, that would be great. Are you feeling ok?"

I tip my head to one side as I look at him, "Um, yes. I'm fine. Why?"

"You don't seem like the type to be so accommodating?"

"Oh! That. Generally, no. But, today I am feeling generous."

With a grin, he asks, "And what has you feeling so generous that you made me food?"

I look away, I know he is teasing but, I am uncomfortable with my reasons. "I feel generous because..." I pause, trying hard to find a way to articulate how or why or something. His hand covers mine on the table causing me to look back at him.

"You don't have to answer. I was only teasing but I can see this isn't comfortable for you. I am grateful for the food. Let's talk about the joining ritual for the pack. Ok?"

I smile at him, grateful. My heart still feels bruised from last night and how do I tell someone that I made food for them because I am just so glad that someone stuck by me. Leonidas and Banner, they are still here. Banner has seen a lot and hasn't even become more, yet. But he is still here. "What is the ritual like? I don't need to kill a goat or something, right?"

Banner chokes on the food he is chewing, coughing and sputtering. He recovers and looks at me, "We do not sacrifice goats! We do eat them, but nothing is sacrificed beyond your ability to be done with our pack. There is a small amount of magic involved, it's a shifter thing. Ours is fancier than most because of my status. That's nothing to worry about though."

"When is it?"

"Two days from now. Two more days and you are part of the pack forever. And technically, part of the world wide pack as well."

"Worldwide? Does that mean I would be subject to pack justice?"

His eyes flash, "What they want is not justice. You will not be subject to that. Ever! They should never have said anything about that to you. It's strange that they did. Either way, you are not under their jurisdiction and I was the one in the room when the body appeared. You were in the middle of a bunch of witnesses. Also, the body did not smell like your magic. At all."

"Because it smelled like burnt oranges and stale coffee and everything that is Hake."

"Yes, but you smell dimensional. This did not smell like that."

"Dimensional? What?"

He slides his chair back and gets up, coming to kneel next to me. He lifts my chair and turns it while setting it back from the table so I am facing him. My heart is racing and parts of me are wide awake and at attention now. He leans in, inhaling deeply. His eyes are closed as he says, "You smell like the earth. Not the scent that people claim is earth. Like all of it. Deserts and dark forests, lakes, oceans, clear mountain air; all of it blended together as one living organism. Wild roses wind their way through it all, and the scent of rain is ever present and moving through it all." His eyes open, they are golden and not human anymore. His voice has gotten deeper while he spoke, "I am going to take you now if you don't walk away."

My breath catches as every fiber in my being welcomes him to do just that. Instead of speaking I lift my hands and run my fingers up his arms, across his shoulders and thread them into his hair, pulling him to me as my legs open to allow him closer. He growls and his arms wrap around me, snatching me up against his body, "You should have run away while you could." His lips on mine and I open for him, his tongue and mine fighting for dominance. We break for air and he kisses a trail of fire down my neck. He gets to my shirt and snatches it up, pulling my hands out of his hair. He stares at my breasts like a starving man and as my hands come down I run them down the tops of them to pull the cups down under them. He takes them in his hands like they are spun sugar, pressing kisses all over them. Heightening my awareness of every inch of skin.

My head tips back with a moan when I feel his hot breath on my nipple. It is painfully tight now as he takes it in his mouth. He sucks hard and grazes it with his teeth. My hands, still on my bra cups release those and move to his still shirt covered chest. His mouth on my other nipple now, my hands curl into his shirt. He lifts his head from my nipple and I tug his shirt up, straightening myself so I can see. He snatches his shirt off and sends it flying. Sweet Lady he is gorgeous and big. His chest is broad and he is not missing any days at the gym. The hair on his chest tapers down to his pants and I can see his cock pushing out through the waistband.

I look up at his still golden eyes, "We should set him free. I'll take off mine if you will do the same?" He is up and snatching his pants down before I can blink. I stand, happy that I am only wearing pajama bottoms today and I tug them down just far enough that I can let them drop to the floor as he struggles to get his shoes off. He notices my pants on the ground and works faster to get the boots off. Being helpful like I am I put one foot up on his chair, my leg bent at the knee. His eyes are on me as I run my fingers up my thigh to slide between the lips of my pussy. He falls over as he snatches his boot off. The other one goes flying when two of my fingers enter my dripping cunt. Suddenly his tongue is circling my clit, he pauses long enough to say, "Fuck yourself till you come on my face." Then he sucks hard on my clit and my core clenches around my fingers. I start pumping them in and out as his tongue works magic on my clit. He reaches up and rolls a nipple between his thumb and finger, that is more than I can take. I cry out as my body convulses with my orgasm. He shoves my hand out of the way and tongue fucks me till the waves slow.

Holding me in place, he stands and picks me up, my legs wrap around him of their own volition. His cock is twitching at my pussy and all I want is for him to fill me with it. He lowers my body, impaling me slowly. "Oh Sweet Lady, yes.

Uuunnnhh." My lips seek out his neck and just before I bite him I remember to ask, "Can I bite you?"

He lifts me slightly and rocks his hips away, "Can I bite you?"

"I'll be mad if you don't."

"There's your answer." He slams into me and I think I might die from the pleasure of it. I bite his neck, drinking lightly from him as he takes me to a bed. He lays me on the bed and just starts fucking me hard and fast. I release his neck, and the holes close even as he bites mine and I come again with a shout, my nails digging into his back. He releases my neck and straightens, I see a little of my blood on his lips before he licks it away. He pulls out and flips me over, entering me from behind. He runs the fingers of one hand down to my clit and starts making slow circles over it as he fucks me. His other hand gathers my hair and pulls me back against him. He whispers in my ear, "Every inch of you tastes so fucking good. You're going to come for me one more time, when I do. Don't you come till I tell you to, understand?"

I nod and moan as he presses my clit. Then he goes back to fucking me hard an fast. His hand on my clit and the other in my hair. He bites the spot where shoulder and neck meet and I am ready to explode. "Oh Gods, I'm going to come!" He fucks me harder and growls at me. "Oh Gods, I can't. I'm— oh fuck me! He lets go of my neck and whispers now in my ear, then slams into me harder, his fingers rubbing my clit as I explode into a million points of light.

When I come to we are both leaned over the bed breathing hard, his cock still pulsing in me. I smile, "You maybe want to do that again?"

He huffs a laugh, "Gods yes."

Twenty-Six

Jasmine

Since we don't want to kill Hake out in the middle of the magical sector, for much the same reasons why Scarlett didn't want to fight me there, we are waiting for him to leave the apartment. I feel it is pretty safe to assume that he has his place heavily trapped. So we really don't want to fuck around in there and risk that. Which means we are back out here, checking on Hake. We have been watching from the alley, but have yet to see him through any of the windows. Leonidas and I have been here for hours already.

"I can't sit here any longer. I'm going to go peek in his window."

Leonidas looks at me like I have grown a second head, "What? No. That is not a good idea. We need to sit here and wait."

"Look, I won't go up on his porch or anything. I just want to go see if there is a better angle that will let me see him."

Leonidas rubs the bridge of his nose with one hand, "Fine. But I want to be on record, this is a bad idea."

"It absolutely is, but I'm going to do it anyway. Thank you for not arguing further." He rolls his eyes at me as I walk across the street. The area has plenty of people wandering about, I am just another one of them... Watching the window I can see best as I walk I am nearly to his stairs when his door opens and wolves come out. I recognize one of them and I freeze at exactly the moment when they spot me. "It's her!" "Get her!"

I spin around and take off running like my life depends on it because it sure as fuck does. I am never going to live this down if I live through this. I am running like the hounds of hell are behind me and well, that isn't far off. The four chasing me don't look great and they are not far behind me. I put on a little more speed as a truck comes up to cruise next to me. Leonidas! He shoves the middle window open, "Jump in!"

I dive into the truck and he takes off, quickly leaving the ones chasing me far behind. I breathe a sigh of relief and sit up. I look at the middle window. No way is any part of me fitting through that. Leonidas puts down the window on the passenger side of the truck. I climb in as we go, real damn grateful to not be just a human right now.

Sitting in the truck, I glance over at him. His hands are tight on the wheel and his face hard. Damn. "You were right and I should have listened to you. I was wrong and nearly got myself killed for it. I'm sorry."

"Dammit Jasmine! You scared the hell out of me. You could have been caught by them. There was four of them, and only two of us. And that doesn't even count Hake in the building! You can't do this to me. I, I don't know what I would do if I lost you."

"I'm so sorry. I didn't take any of that into account. I should have. I can't promise I won't do something dumb again. I can promise to try harder to keep myself alive and not hurt you that way."

He chuckles, "You know, the first time I saw you I thought you would be the best trouble I ever got into. Standing there, so human. So fragile. Bruises all over that most people would never see. When you left with Mikael that night I stayed in your trailer. I looked around and I could smell your blood everywhere. I knew he had beat you, and that somehow you still had the strength to defy me, knowing that I had a hand in killing the one that had been hurting you for so long. I knew that night that I had to do anything in my power to get close to you. A woman that could still be completely defiant in the face of what must have seemed like certain death, that was someone that I needed to know better. All this, and though you scared me and I never want to experience that again, I guess I can understand. Your daily life for a long time was just a big game of Russian roulette. You never knew if you would make it through the day. So maybe I need to ease up. How many people in your life, before now, have ever given a single fuck about whether or not you survived the day?"

Oh hell. I did not study for this. "Um, well. My parents. They are the only ones I can think of that cared before I entered this life." And they died when I was still so young. I don't think they would recognize any part of me now. I swallow the lump in my throat and I look out the window so he doesn't see the tears I am furiously blinking away.

"I thought as much." He sighs. "Ok. So, first, I forgive

you. I can't expect you to be thinking about things you've never had to worry about. Things that were so far outside your experience of life as to be nonexistent. Please try to keep us in mind when you figure your risk acceptance ratios. Second, I think maybe you need tacos."

Holy shit. Did he just say he understood and forgave me? What universe am I in that this is happening? I am going with it, he said tacos and I could eat. "Thank you and fuck yeah tacos! Where are we going?"

He laughs, a real one with his beautiful smile. "I know where a truck parks, some of my crews go to it on the regular. They love it, I am betting you will too."

Grinning, I tell him, "Only one way to find out."

Ten minutes later we are sitting under a tree with a spread of tacos in a box. Leonidas is sitting in front of the tree, leaned against it. His tough exterior on full display in his white undershirt and jeans. His legs stretched out before him ending in work boots scuffed and well used, shirt tucked into a back pocket. He doesn't feel the heat or the cold but pretends to it like I do. His eyes behind the sunglasses continually scan the area around us, so I decide not to worry for once. I am just going to sit here and eat my damn tacos. They smell amazing. The ladies running the place thought I should get the not spicy versions, I can feel their eyes on me as I take a bite of the first taco.

The spices fill my mouth with flavor and heat. I am in love. The first taco is gone in a few bites and I proceed through the rest with the same fervor. Somewhere around halfway through the box the women stop watching me. Leonidas, still scanning, never really stops watching me. "Do you miss eating," I ask between bites.

"Not really. I did for the first ten years or so but then I

just didn't anymore. Now, I feed pretty regular on people that no one is sorry about them being gone. I was less picky when I was running a gang and had less regard for getting caught."

"Ah, so it was never about whether it was right to kill someone, only whether there would be a consequence?"

"Essentially. As I see it, there is no one on this planet that hasn't a death on their hands. My only concern was where I could feed a crowd with less concern for repercussion. A ratty trailer park burns to the ground, the owner might get fined for the faulty repairs that led to it but no one is going to look closely at whether or not the poor that lived there died because of the fire or something else."

"I guess you mean because people eat other creatures to live and that is what you are doing. I can understand that." My tacos are gone and I put my hands on the ground behind me so I can lean back. "Since we know he is there, maybe we need to go back tonight and see if we can collect him up. While the bar is loud. Especially since it would appear he is working with Frank's pack."

He looks at me through the shades, "I think you are right. I'll tell everyone tonight is a night off after a quick guard duty and I am buying the drinks for the night. Banner can come with us. The rest will be at the bar, but arriving only a little before us and knowing they may need to fight."

That night

.   .   .

Leonidas, Banner and I arrive back at Hake's place. Unlike with the books, I check for traps this time and I find them. So many. It seems like it takes forever to untie them all. When I am done it has only been thirty minutes. We creep in and though we can smell that he was here, there is nothing fresh like he is here now. I sweep the place for more traps before we really check the place out.

He left very little, though he did leave me a note on the counter. I read it out loud to the guys, "My dearest Jasmine, I am touched you would try to see me. Our time will come but for now, you will have to content yourself with all the traps I left for you. Did you find the one on this note before you picked it up?" I laugh, "Ha! Yes, I did you shady fuck. Where was I? Oh, here. If you didn't, well, I'm sure you'll get out in a few days. Do look for my invitation to arrive. See you soon. Yours, Hake."

"Asshole." I look over when Leonidas speaks, "I hope I get to see you take his stupid head off. Don't give him the pleasure of being bitten by you."

Banner nods, "Agreed. No bites for that asshole. But maybe I can hold him for you and you can kick his head for a goal? I bet I could get the guys to set up a net real quick."

Leonidas grins, "I would be willing to help with that."

I roll my eyes at the two of them, "Come on. Let's get out of here."

Twenty-Seven

JASMINE

Today is the day I officially join Banner's pack. I am excited and kind of nervous that maybe the pack won't like me. Banner had to go home last night to prepare some things. Leonidas stayed with me so I had plenty to keep me occupied and not thinking too much about this. I am in the kitchen having coffee and talking to him when Banner walks in with a large white box. I am immediately suspicious that there are things I haven't been told about this ritual. Leonidas' smirk confirms my suspicion. "Banner, what is that?"

He smiles but looks very nervous, "It's a dress. For the ritual. Which might be a little more fancy than I led you to believe."

Getting up from my chair I take my coffee to the counter and set it down. Turning back to Banner I tell him, "Put the box on the table and open it. Let me see just what you might have left out."

He sets the box down as Leonidas walks over to me and

puts an arm around me, giving me a squeeze and murmuring, "Go easy on him. There are a lot of things he has no choice in because of who he was born to be."

Well shit. Now I can't even be upset with him. I watch as Banner lifts the lid off the box. The dress is dark blue and simple, though elegant. He lifts the dress out of the box, "I can get you a different one if you don't like this one. You can pick whatever you like. But this is going to be a much more official occasion than I had hoped to have so, we kind of have to dress for the occasion. You too, Leonidas."

Leonidas looks surprised at that, "I didn't think I would be invited?"

Banner shrugs, "It's not like she can have an important day without both of us being there."

Crossing the room I touch the dress. It is soft and silky to the touch along the bodice and halfway down the skirt tiny little sparkles start appearing. By the hem it is filled with them. The spaghetti straps and deep vee manage to keep the top simple and the overall effect stunning. I look up at him, "You picked this out for me?" He nods, biting his lower lip. "I'll wear it. Now what haven't you told me? Or should I ask what changed?"

Banner heaves a sigh of relief, "Um, it would have been kept simple but, hmm. Someone leaked it to my parents. And then they leaked more to them and now they are coming too." He sets the dress down carefully in the box, "And they have to approve all of this now." He shoves a hand through his hair. "I'm sorry. I was trying to do this quietly and that just didn't happen. I'm going to find out who is on their payroll and send them to Greenland."

"Oh dear. And what happens when they don't like me? I mean, can they forbid you seeing me? Are you going to have to break up with me?" Another thought occurs to me, "Will I not be able to join the pack?"

Banner steps over and wraps his arms around me, "No! You will become part of the pack. That isn't up for debate at all. They very much agree you will be a valuable addition to the pack."

I look up at him, "Then what?"

He sighs and his cheeks flush, "They are coming to decide if you will be a good fit for the family. They are not overly happy about Leonidas, but only because he is a vampire. Sorry, Leonidas, old beliefs and all that."

Leonidas chuckles, "Don't worry about it. I probably wouldn't be thrilled about adding me to my family by proxy either."

"But you, you are a different creature all together and they feel that they should make their own evaluation. Word of you has spread. Mostly from people that—" his eyes flash and he looks away. He swallows and clears his throat, or maybe he is just growling softly. "People that are not worth the time it would take to hunt them. So, they would like to verify that you are not as has been reported."

"What are they saying? Do people think I have multiple heads? Disfigured? Wait, I know." I pull away from him to pace, "They must be telling people that I am poisonous to everyone now and that I feed exclusively on others in the magical community. Or perhaps I fly around killing everything in sight on the dark of the moon?"

Leonidas snags my arm and pulls me into his. "You know we don't believe any of that. Give it time, people will come around. You are new, a creature that would not, could not be in the normal course of things. Even magical people dislike change. In fact, I would say that we dislike it more even, because we tend toward a longer view of things. You, my beautiful vixen, are a hella big change. Until they get adjusted, try not to kill anyone. Pretty sure that will make it take longer. Or less time. This is not the point. You should definitely not kill anyone today. Today, you put on the pretty dress that Banner brought you. Get a nice pair of heels from the creature in your walls. Are they still stealing your shoes?"

I shake my head no, "They stopped when I started leaving offerings."

Banner laughs, "They were holding your shoes hostage for offerings?"

I shrug, "Yeah. Tea and honey. In a little tea set. After that, my shoes stayed lined up. Oh, cookies too."

Leonidas hums, "Can't forget the cookies. It isn't tea without the biscuits. I think that one came home from across the pond with my mother. But it could have been a dream. She always said that it was a good creature, and should never have been treated the way it was. I was a teen, so I didn't listen to a lot of what she said."

I rest my head on Leonidas' chest for a moment. "They are going to hate me. Why are they so concerned about adding me anyway? Maybe we should skip all this. Do I really need to be in a pack?"

Banner grabs a chair and sits in it. "I did not want to tell you this. It feels really presumptuous to even say it so, I'm really sorry." I peek over at him through the curtain of my hair as he continues. His face is bright red, "One of the things the informant told them is that I have been pursuing you exclusively for sometime. They apparently noticed that I erm. Was not sleeping with anyone else anymore. Oh gods this sucks."

"Keep going. Please."

His face lifts, an almost smile plays on his lips, "They are curious if you could be my um, hmm…" he rushes through the last two words, "my mate."

He suddenly finds his hands very interesting as I turn to look at him, "So this isn't about me being accepted into the pack. They want to know if I am your mate? And they know about Leonidas? They aren't expecting me to ditch him, right?"

He shakes his head no without looking up, "No, other than annoyed that he is a vampire, multiple men aren't a concern in our world. Women aren't as prevalent as men because for the most part, we are big on consent as whole. No one wants to give a woman a reason to kill them and the ability to do so with ease."

Not willing to let Leonidas go but feeling the need to offer comfort to Banner, I tug him over with me. I run my hand over his hair, "I guess I understand that. And I wouldn't be mad about being mated to you and Leonidas."

"You wouldn't?" They ask in unison.

"No, I wouldn't. Leonidas has proven over and over that he is here no matter what. You were with me as I turned into a wholly different creature and you found a way to comfort me that I was able to sense even as I was sure I would die in pain. Through it all neither of you has decided I am an abomination or frightening. You are both really kind to me. Understanding when I nearly get myself killed and scare the hell out of you." Leonidas leans down to rest his head on my shoulder and wraps an arm around my ribs. "You both have done your best to take care of me even as I have fumbled madly at figuring out how to accept that care. All the while, following my lead and trying to go with whatever flow I happen to be on. I could, and have, done so much worse. I feel pretty lucky even if being mated to anyone kind of frightens me the way me almost dying frightens you guys."

Banner's arms slip round my hips and he rests his forehead on my belly, "Thank you."

"What? I didn't do anything."

I am still looking down at him, confused when he lifts his head and brings his face close to mine, "For being you. For not running away from all of this. For choosing my pack. But mostly for being you." He closes the space between us, pressing his lips to mine. I am lost in the sweetness of it. His lips move with mine, the kiss deepens. Leonidas traces the underside of my breast, his other hand coming to rest on my shoulder as he trails little bites to my neck. My pussy is suddenly throbbing and the idea of having these two men in my bed at the same time has me dripping wet and needy.

I break the kiss, "We don't, we don't have to be there anytime soon, right? How long do we have?"

His eyes are golden as he watches Leonidas's hands pinch and twirl my nipples through the oversize shirt I am wearing for a nightgown, "Not for hours yet. The limo won't be here till this evening. We have the whole day to... prepare."

Leonidas straightens and presses against my backside, his cock digging into my back through his jeans. His fingers begin bunching the shirt I am wearing, lifting it an inch at a time to reveal my lack of clothing underneath it. Banner groans and drops to his knees in front of me as Leonidas lifts the shirt over my head. He tosses it somewhere and his hands come back to my breast as Banner's tongue slips between my lips to flick at my clit. I moan as everything flutters. I hear a zipper and Leonidas' cock is pressing against my back. I reach behind myself to grasp it, stroking my thumb back and forth over the edge where shaft ends and head begins. He presses into my hands as his fingers pinch my nipples. Banner spreads my lips with his fingers, his tongue making slow circles on my clit. Leonidas takes my hand from his cock and moves it to Banner's head. My fingers thread into his hair of their own volition as he puts a light suction on my clit. I feel Leonidas lining up with my entrance and I moan as my core quivers with anticipation. He presses in slowly and the feeling of one man sucking my clit while another's cock enters me is amazing. He holds himself in place for a moment after he is fully encased in my hot, quivering sheath.

I feel Leonidas's hands trace down the curves of my body to my hips, he grasps them firmly and starts fucking me hard and fast. Both my hands are twined in Banner's hair, holding on for all I'm worth as he sucks harder on my clit. I am soaring with pleasure, my entire body on fire. My breath catches and I cry out as my body starts twitching and convulsing with an orgasm for the ages. I yank Banner's head away from my clit when I just can't take the sensation overload anymore. He rises up and takes my breasts in his hands, kissing me deeply as his fingers pinch my nipples. Leonidas fucks me harder, the waves of my orgasm just keep coming in with his cock. He slams into me and holds himself there, shouting my name. No sooner does he slide out than Banner lifts me up to impale me on his cock, his hands going to my ass to lift and hold me up. My legs and arms wrap around his body, ankles hooking behind him even as my nails dig into his back. My hair is swept up into a bunch in Leonidas's hand, he bites one side of my neck causing my whole body to shiver as I moan. I can feel another orgasm building as his fingers slip between us to rub my clit, slow at first but faster with each circle. Banner, never slowing his pace, leans his head in to the other side of my neck and bites me. It's more than I can take as another orgasm rips through my body. Banner speeds up and shortly is slamming into me to hold himself still as he pulses within me. The two of them release the bites they had on either side of my neck, kissing the spots as they heal over.

I am just slipping on my shoes when Leonidas comes to tell me that the limo has arrived. I turn and his eyes travel down my body and back up, a low rumble of a growl coming from his chest as his eyes darken with hunger.

"Sir, we need to get going. We can talk about your opinion of the dress when we get back," I tell him as I slip past him and walk toward the front door.

He follows along behind me saying, "You know, we didn't ask how long the limo ride would be."

"I am not meeting his parents reeking of sex. That is why I insisted we all shower. You will just need to wait until we finish our business this evening. Then we can talk about what pops up." Banner's eyes widen as he catches what I am saying, then this wolfish grin crosses his face and he opens the door of the limo for me.

I get in and have a seat facing the front of the limo. Leonidas stops to ask Banner, just how long is this ride. They are both striking in their tuxes and I could watch them pretty content for a while. Banner tells him the ride will be less than twenty minutes and he sighs. They both get in and we are off. My heart rate picks up. Did he answer me about what happens if his parents don't like me? He didn't. Oh shit. What if they don't? "Banner, what happens if they don't like me? You never answered that question."

Banner stares out the window, "Let's leave that for if it comes up, okay?"

I don't like the look on his face, how bad is it if he won't even tell me before hand? I leave it alone. He is obviously bothered by the thought of it and tonight is supposed to be a good night. The car slows and I look out the window. We are going to a whole damn castle. Get the fuck out of here. How the hell did they hide this so close in to Durham? This is an entire estate. The drive is long and winding and there appears to be a ton of people here. Holy fuck.

Banner taps his leg with one hand as our limo waits in line to drop us at the door. It gets faster and faster until he turns to look at us, "Listen. They are going to make a big fuss over us as we arrive. Crown prince and guests, you know. So. Yeah. Jasmine, for the protocol here, I get out, you get out, Leonidas gets out. You put your arm in mine and then in Leonidas's. We all walk slowly in together, got it?"

"Yes. It needs to be you first here because appearances. We must present a united front and seem smoothly practiced. Got it." We pull up in front and all my nervous energy dissipates like it never was. The door is opened and Banner gets out, followed by myself and Leonidas. I wait until both men are standing with me and slip my hand onto their arms one after the other like we had done it a million and one times already. The flashes going off constantly were not something I expected but that's fine. We walk sedately in, pausing when asked for pictures. It is strange that so many people would wait out here just to get pictures but, I guess it is what it is. Inside the flashes are gone and quiet music plays. A man in a suit appears before us, "Prince Banner, your presence and that of your guests is requested in the drawing room by their highnesses the King and Queen, your parents."

Banner nods so regally I am a little weirded out by it. But as we follow the man to the drawing room he gives my hand a light squeeze. The man opens the double doors to the drawing room and announces, "Crown Prince Banner and his... guests." The pause was so tiny, almost not a pause but intentionally just barely a pause. Super. Those kind of people.

Inside the room, seated on a loveseat, are the king and queen. Banner's parents. He doesn't release my arm to go to hug them and I am shocked. How can you have living parents that you don't hate but don't go hug when you see them?

Banner stiffens and says, "Mother, Father. Very nice to see you again. I would like to introduce you to my companions, Jasmine and Leonidas."

I do a small curtsy and Leonidas gives a cursory bow. The king and queen nod, while continuing to look us over. I know this means a lot to Banner so I don't tell them anything about how rude they are. Just as my patience is beginning to fray the king says, "Please, sit." He gestures at the only other seating in the room, another loveseat. Meant for only two people.

Banner looks at the seat then his parents. His eyes narrow and he guides us over, he and Leonidas sit and then tug me down to sit on them, each providing a leg as chair. Of course now all I can see is his parents. They look as though they are recalling stepping in shit recently. The queen lets a little sigh escape then asks, "Jasmine, where did you grow up? I don't recall you in any of the gatherings I have seen."

"That is because I grew up human. I was fully human until a year ago." Banner's hand is on my back, I wish we had worked out signals before hand instead of having mad sex. Well, maybe in addition to having mad sex.

His father's mouth twists, "Well, who were your parents? We know a great many humans as well."

"My parents have been dead for most of my life. I grew up with my aunt. I am pretty sure she isn't someone you knew. I doubt you go to the right church for one." Banner makes a small noise and his fingers press into my back.

The queen's mouth twists, I can't tell if it is disgust or humor. She says, "What exactly are you now? You are no longer human and I hear rumors of strange things. Things that shouldn't be and are possibly dangerous."

Damn. They had to go there. "Well, I became a vampire and not long after that found that in addition to becoming a vampire I had absorbed powers that were always meant for me. Very recently some wolf shifters from a certain pack decided to poison me with their blood at a restaurant. I nearly died but my friends were able to save me and I became wolf shifter too. So now I am all of those things. As for shouldn't be, well, it is my understanding that Hekate very much hoped that I would become exactly this however it happened so I guess you will need to take up should or shouldn't be with her."

The queen seems to be smirking but the king looks apoplectic. His face is bright red and I wonder if he is going to shift and try to attack us. He splutters, "How dare you!"

Banner taps my back twice and I stand, hoping that is what he meant. A half step forward and the two of them stand in unison behind me. Banner steps neatly around me to stand between his parents and I as his father stands, saying, "Banner, I cannot believe you brought this upstart, gold digging twit—"

"Father, you want to watch what you say. I don't care who the rest of the world see you as. You will not speak about Jasmine this way. Especially when you are so very wrong. She didn't know I am royalty until very recently, she was already becoming part of the pack at that point and I had been pursuing her for quite some time. As for gold-digging, well, she didn't know I had money either. But I was well aware that she had plenty. If anything, it appeared that I was the gold digger."

The queen stands then, having watched all this, "Howard, that is enough." He turns to growl at her and she slaps him so hard his head rocks back.

Leonidas giggles, whispering in my ear, "Mom slapped dad in the drawing room."

The queen raises a brow as though she heard, a corner of her mouth lifting. "I said that is enough Howard. She isn't as we heard or it would have been her that lost her temper, not you. You and I both know she has a ridiculous amount of money and we probably know more about her parents than she does. Now, remember who you are or I will punish you tonight."

The king looks stricken, "No! Don't make me sleep alone! Anything but that!"

Banner groans, "Oh for fuck's sake. Can you please not play your gross games here? At least wait till we leave the room? Jasmine, Leonidas, I'm so sorry."

Leonidas and I giggle, I pat Banner's back, "Don't worry, we are thoroughly entertained."

"Great. Just great. Thanks parents. More trauma." Banner says as he shakes his head and turns away from his parents. One hand rubbing his eyes he says, "I tried to bleach my eyes once because of this. Hurts like hell. Does not in fact erase the image. Healing took a solid week. The benefit to that was no lessons that week and my parents avoided playing their games in front of me for a blissful six weeks. Six thousand years would not have been long enough and yet, here we are. Are they done yet?"

Leonidas laughs, "They are not done and I feel like we should not have concerned ourselves with what they would think if we showed up smelling like sex. I think they need some time alone. Ew. You grew up with this? That explains a lot."

Banner groans. "That's it. Let's go. Jasmine, if you like me at all, lead me to the door. I'll open my eyes on the other side of it."

I look toward his parents thinking it can't be that bad. They wouldn't. Not in front of their son and people they—. Oh. They would. Oh my. I pull Banner toward the door and Leonidas is on the other side of him looking just as wildly uncomfortable as Banner and I. We get outside the door and there are two guys standing there. They take one look at our faces and say, "Oh dear. Come, we'll take you to a room where you can refresh."

The quiet one stayed behind, turning and putting his back to the door as the one speaking led us down the hall.

Twenty-Eight

JASMINE

The employees of the King and Queen brought us drinks and snacks in the other room. We stayed there for a little while, just till we thought we could pretend we had not seen terrible things.

Then Banner stood up and said, "It's time. We need to introduce you to some more of the pack. You have only met a fraction of them. Same drill as walking in, we all stick together and you must keep things balanced between he and I tonight.Only for while my parents are here. When we are with just our pack, it won't matter."

I nod and we spent what seemed like forever wandering the large ballroom introducing Leonidas and myself to everyone there. Finally, we seem to have met everyone we can meet and then this bell rings throughout the crowd. It is light and has a pleasant tinkling sound to it, I am surprised the sound travels so readily through the noise of the gather-ing.People begin moving into what seems to be prearranged places and Banner guides us toward the front of the room where a small group of people are waiting. His parents are part of the group so apparently they are finished. Hopefully they can refrain until all this is done. Banner suddenly tenses as we draw near the group. I whisper, "What's wrong?"

Banner is pale as he whispers back, "My parents have double crossed us. They brought the priest to marry us. If we say no right now it will cause an issue and will mean that we cannot be together in the future. If we go through with it, we are bound. Marriage here is forever. Whether we like it or not. And in this case, they mean to include you Leonidas. I think that is how they mean to prevent this from happening."

Leonidas grins, "I am tied to her anyway. Let's do it and really fuck'em up."

I look at him, my eyes wide, "Really? You're okay with this?"

"Yeah," he shrugs, "I told you, I am here. However that looks."

I look over to Banner, "And you? How do you feel about this?"

He frowns, "I hate that my parents are forcing this choice on us right now. That pisses me off and I want to do terrible things. But at the same time, I have no doubts about the ceremony with you two. I knew I wanted to keep you from the first day I met you."

I look back at the group we are closing in on, "Let's do this."

We stop a few paces away from the group. The King smiles at us but there is no warmth in his smile, "Welcome everyone," his voice booms out over the crowd. "We are delighted to be here and to officiate the bonding of our son to the one that most are calling abomination. We think she will be a fine addition to the pack and to our fearsome reputation. She has even tamed a vampire!" I can hear the gasps and groans of the people behind me, mutters of what the hell. I am not sure exactly whether they are sympathetic or appalled. My lovers are shaking with rage on either side of me as the King continues to say awful things about us couched in polite speak. Pressing my fingertips into each of their arms, I can only hope they get my message. I have dealt with so many like this asshole King before me.

He wants for nothing more than to goad us into an attack and then he can claim we are violent and must be imprisoned. More likely though he would imprison Leonidas and myself, in hopes of forcing Banner to do whatever it is that he has refused to do thus far. The King wraps up his speech and three officers of Banner's pack come to stand before us, their eyes speak volumes as to how they feel about the things said and I offer them a small smile. They clasp each others hands and ours, creating a small circle with the six of us. The one across from me says, "Jasmine, you did not become a wolf of your own free will. Do you choose to become part of this pack of your own free will?"

As he speaks a golden mist seems to rise from us, surrounding us. "Yes, I freely choose to become a part of Banner's pack."

"You agree that this pack, and only this pack, will be your family. The ones to whom ties run deeper than mere blood?"

I had questioned this when Banner told me about it, I was worried I wouldn't be able to claim others as family, adopting them into my community. He assured me that this was specific to other wolf packs and my fears soothed I have no problem responding, "This pack is the family I choose, to whom I accept ties deeper than blood."

The golden mist swirls around us, obscuring us from the view of the others. The one before me says, "By the Goddess Hekate, we are joined as family, as pack. Your cause is ours and ours is yours."

The mist is near a solid wall of spun gold right now, and Hekate appears in the middle of us. She smiles warmly at me and turns a slow circle. The people from the pack are more than a little awed as they stand there, when she is facing me again she says, "You have done well. This, this will be good for my favorite pack, They can use the shake up in leadership." She looks at Banner, "Your time is coming sooner than you would like. Make me proud again." He nods and she looks to Leonidas, "Your mother sends her love. You are a credit to her in so many ways. You, keep the faith and, guard her well. That goes for both of you." She looks back to me, "I am so proud of you. This is going to work out for you, so much better than that asshole father of Banner's could possibly imagine. Enjoy it the best you can under the circumstances. Know that I am always watching."

"Hmm, I hope not always, always...." I cannot believe Leonidas said that, but Hekate laughs. She disappears, along with the golden mist that dissipates much slower.

The ones that did the ceremony with us bow, Banner and Leonidas return the bow while I do a quick curtsy. I fucking hate curtsies. They return to their places while the priest comes to stand before us. The priest clears his throat, "This is all very outside the ordinary. I haven't met with any of you and there is a vampire. Do vampires even bond?"

He looks very old and very confused by all this. I slip my hand from my lovers arms and I step forward, taking one of his hands between mine, "I am so sorry this was thrust on you like this. I can promise you that we all very much wish this, no matter the circumstance surrounding it. As for vampires, yes. They bond to others."

He smiles and lifts his eyes to look into mine. His eyes, they look almost familiar... Then he squints, "Well, now that's settled, get back over there and we'll get started."

Walking back over to where they stand I take my place, hands back on their arms and the priest begins the ceremony. "Bonding is a decision not to be made lightly. Forever has a different ring to it when it means hundreds of years with the same person."

He goes on about choices and knowing what you are getting into but I am stuck on that first part. Hundreds of years with the same person. That is terrifying and at the same time ignites a deep yearning to have someone that would love me for that long. I glance at Banner and Leonidas on either side of me. They are both kind and good and they strive to understand me. They don't try to control me, even when they are concerned I am likely to get myself killed. They have stuck with me when no one except Hekate has. More importantly, none of us are trapped, exactly. I mean, we will always want to be close to the others, but we aren't financially trapped with each other.

I take a deep breath. I think I am really okay with this. I love these two and I know they love me. I tune in to what the priest is saying again just in time to hear my name, "Jasmine, will you claim these men as yours?" As he says the words a lovely line of red mist extends from his hands to ours, stopping before it touches us, as though waiting for my answer.

"I will claim these men as mine."

The magic weaves around my arms, not yet including the men. The priest asks them, "Do you, Banner and Leonidas, do you claim this woman?"

They answer together, "I claim this woman." The magic wraps around their arms, weaving their arms to mine. The priest makes a little twist with his hands and the magic cuts off from him and sinks into our arms, leaving the faintest of lines on our skin. He throws up his arms and proclaims loudly for the room, "It is done! The crown prince is mated! Now we celebrate!" Cheers resound throughout the room, so loud it hurts my ears. I glance over to his parents, they don't look as happy as they should for people that just got exactly what they seemed to want. The priest insists we turn and be greeted by this huge line of people that has suddenly formed behind us. Holy shit. Where were they hiding all those gifts? I glance over at Banner, he smiles sheepishly and shrugs. I can't help but smile.

"Did you know they would do this?" He nods, and I look over at Leonidas, "I think we need to expand on the house. So we can fit all the stuff."

They both laugh and Leonidas says, "We can expand the house. We should probably make it our own anyway and since we are all tied together now... Maybe we should all live in the same house."

"Maybe we should at that." The first person is allowed to come up and greet us then, effectively cutting off our conversation.

The next morning

I can't believe I am bound to two men and we are all just sitting in the kitchen doing morning things. Banner and I with our coffee and Leonidas the blood kept in the fridge, it all just seems so normal. When I was human and married to a human, I never had this level of normalcy.

Banner and Leonidas are discussing plans for the house when my phone goes off. I see it's Jan and my heart starts racing. I take another sip of my coffee and answer the phone, "Hello Jan, how are you?"

"I am well, thanks. I hope you are too. Listen, I'm not going to beat around the bush here. We talked about continuing your lessons. We all agree that we want to, you are amazing. At the same time, we all want to live and that is why we cannot continue to teach you. Besides, your defensive and offensive magics are well past the point of needing our training. The smaller basics that you still are working on, you will learn those with time and you could always do some reading from the library that doesn't exist that you don't have anything to do with."

My jaw drops, "You all know about that?"

She says, "That library is the worst kept secret in the magical community. Though most don't have the slightest idea of how to find it or who guards it. A few of us know now who guards it, only because it came to us as we did readings on what we should do. We were that divided about it. And I mean we were each of us divided in that we all wanted to continue but wanted to live."

I nod like she can see me before I remember I am on the

phone, "No, I understand. I want you all to live long, happy lives too. Thank you for letting me know."

"Thank you for understanding. Don't be a stranger at the book store. We would still like to see you socially, if you are ok with that."

Smiling I say, "You couldn't tear me away. See you soon." Tapping end call I look up to find Banner and Leonidas watching me. "I guess you heard that."

They nod, Leonidas says, "We need to finish this so you can live."

"I was thinking we could do another spell to find him, but when we are ready to go."

Banner sets his cup on the table, "We should bring the pack. They won't appreciate being left out of this."

Leonidas gets up and rinses his glass, "I think we should bring the pack too. We know he is working with Frank's pack and he may have them wherever he is hiding. He knows we are going to look for him." Turning to lean against the counter he continues, "He won't however, expect us to bring reinforcements. Not because we haven't before. Because we haven't since Mikael died. He was a rogue player and we didn't see him coming till after he had already been in the library. Since then it has mostly been us reacting, very little planning."

I look to my coffee as if it will provide answers. It remains still, its surface undisturbed by the turmoil within me. "I don't like it. I don't like asking people that just met me to risk their lives for me." I can see both of them are prepping their arguments so I hurry to say, "While I don't like it, I think you are right."

Banner starts with, "Look, this is what family— Wait. Did you agree?"

Leonidas chuckles, "She did big bad wolf. Stow that argument for another day." He walks over to me, kneels down next to me and says, "Before we start all that, how about we go get dirty and then clean up in the shower? The big bad wolf can come too." He laughs, "Get it? He can come too?" I can't help but giggle even as Banner rolls his eyes.

Twenty-Nine

I message Nia, asking her if she will cast the spell to find Hake again. She sends back that she'll meet me in the library in five. I look over to Banner, one eyebrow raised. He says, "They'll be here by the time we finish."

I nod and lead the way to the door of the library. Pulling the key out of my pocket I unlock it, walking through the door I am still amazed by this place. I can only hope that this isn't the last time I see it. There are so many books I have yet to read, that would be tragic. Shaking off the melancholy I stride into the main area. Demetris stands before me, "You can't do this. The library needs you. You are taking foolish risks."

"You know as well as I do that killing Hake is what I was ordered to do. It has to happen. Just because I fucked up getting to him doesn't mean that I get a pass on it. Just like you, I have a job to do. And the library is your responsibility, just because I have agreed to take on the job of it does not take it from your shoulders. It only gives you reprieve for as long as I am able to take it on."

Demetris gets in my face and yells, "You are needed! The world needs you in it! If I have to lock you away in this library, you are not risking your life to go after Hake!"

Banner and Leonidas grab him up by the arms and take him across the room, even as he shouts that he will take them out if they don't let go of him right now. Nia walks in then, I cast protections over my loves. Demetris shouts, "Your protections won't help them when I tear them to shreds!" They keep him pinned to the wall as I wonder why he hasn't shifted. He is so worked up, he keeps talking about tearing them apart. What exactly is wrong with him?

"Nia, do you see anything off about Demetris?"

She walks over and studies him as he shouts and struggles, Banner and Leonidas easily holding him in place. She reaches out and touches his face, one fingertip to his forehead. The illusion drops and it is just one of the wolves from Frank's pack. She looks back at me, her face drawn with concern, "What did they do with Demetris?"

I can't even begin to imagine so instead I get the chair and the chains they used to try to restrain me. Setting the chair down and waiting while they force him into the chair. Once he is placed in the chair I throw the chains at him, using magic to set them in place and replace the links I got rid of when I escaped them.

The wolf snarls at me. Ignoring that I ask, "Where is Demetris?"

The wolf laughs at me, "You'll have to ask Hake, if you manage to find him, murderer." Leonidas hits the wolf, rocking him in the chair and splashing blood on Banner.

Leonidas says, "Shit man, sorry about that."

Banner laughs, "It's all good, he deserved it and it won't be the last time today I have blood on my clothes."

For my part, I nod. "Murderer? So you think I killed Frank in that horrible manner and you are going to call me names? Fine. Guys, if he twitches, well, do as you please with him." Turning away from him I head for the table where Nia is setting up. "Thank you for coming to do this again. And for getting rid of his glamour. How did you do that? If you don't mind sharing?"

Nia smiles, "I think you'll like this one. I found out by accident many years ago that if you stab into someone wearing a glamour with your magic, it will break the glamour entirely. It doesn't matter where. I found out because my brother used to glamour himself as our father and force me to do a lot of things I shouldn't have been doing. I'd had suspicions for quite some time and I decide to check his mind with a spear of my magic. The illusion crumbled and revealed my brother sitting there smirking at me. Nothing ever happened to him for that. They said I should never have fallen for it and so I was the one at fault. I was a child then. Perhaps thirteen? It has been many years since it happened. I remember it so clearly because that was the day I knew I would not stay a part of that family."

"Shit Nia, I'm sorry."

"Oh no, don't be. Escaping that life has given me freedom, and allowed me to live a life that would be forbidden to me were I still a part of that society."

"I wonder how often your kind leave your society? You are the second elf I have met that has nothing to do with their society."

Her eyes get wide and her hands still, "The second?"

"Yes, the second. The other was Alena's lawyer, Steven Rinfell. Did you not know he is an elf?"

"No, I never paid him any attention. He is an elf? Why

would I not be able to feel that near me at the funeral? I must find out how he hides himself so well. I wonder if he is using something to cause people to ignore him..." She shakes her head, "That is for later. Now, I am ready." She glances back at the wolf in the chair and lowers her voice, "Luckily we still have the map here."

I nod, "Indeed. Well, let's do the thing. The faster we get this finished the better since we also need to find Demetris now."

She lifts her arms to begin and the wolf across the room calls out in a singsong voice, "Oh Miss Murd—" The chair he is in rocks back and slowly tips, crashing to the floor after Banner backhands him before he can finish the word.

Leonidas claps, "Very nice form, maybe a little less force next time. Only so we don't have to continually pick him up off the floor. Or we could brace the chair from behind so you can hit him as hard as you like and the chair doesn't tip."

Banner crosses his arms over his chest, "Better to brace the chair. Or we could take his head off and the whole thing would be a lot less offensive."

The wolf on the floor shouts, "Are you fuckers going to stand me back up?"

My lips twist as I try not to laugh. I start to walk toward them and stop, "Nia, go ahead with the spell. I will be back over in a moment. I'm going to see what this silly fuck wants." She nods and I walk over to where the wolf is sitting upright now and the guys are working to wedge a chair in behind him. "What is your name wolf?"

He looks surprised to be asked that but replies, "Kevin. My name is Kevin."

"Well, Kevin, you were trying to call me over with your rude names. What do you want?"

His eyes narrow as he studies me, "Why are you being so nice to me?"

My brows raise as I ask, "Would you prefer I ask them to hit you some more?" He shakes his head no quickly at that and I ask, "Then call it curiosity as to why you called me."

He sneers, "So you admit to being a murderer then?"

My eyes roll of their own accord, "No stupid. You aren't gaslighting me. If you have something to actually say, then I will come back. For now, I leave you to their tender mercies," I tell him as I gesture to Banner and Leonidas, turning back to Nia and the spell she works for me. I come alongside the table as she finishes the spell. The map blurs as it zooms into a spot. The tiny rock laying on the map rolls across, coming to rest on a place at a crossroads. "No shit. A crossroads. Hekate must be laughing her ass off about that." I hear Kevin yelp but ignore it to study the map. Nia leans in to study the area, "What luck, he ran away to a secluded area in the woods. Much less chance of being caught, or maybe that is his angle too. Much less chance of him getting caught using Kevin's pack to capture your lovers and using them and Demetris to control you. When you go out there, be a sneaky bitch. Don't let him catch those two. Obviously you can't let Kevin go either. And you know... I just thought of something." She turns and looks at Kevin who is very focused on our conversation. "That's what I thought." She flings something out of her hands and black smoke appears around Kevin's head. He starts shouting about not being able to see or hear anything and Nia snaps her fingers, cutting off the sound from him to us as well. I can see his throat working, so he still thinks he is shouting. "So, anyway. I realized that whoever glamoured him may have been watching through his eyes, listening. So, now I want to alter my original statement. Go in there bold and fuck him up. Nosy bastard. I'll babysit this fuck and I'm going to have fun with it. He is going to see all sorts of illusions playing."

Laughing I ask her, "Is he about to get a wholly different version of what is happening here?"

She grins, "If they are watching what they think is you having an orgy here in the library, they sure are not going to be expecting you to bust down the door will they?"

I laugh hard at that, "You are magnificent. Ok. Guys, let's go. We have a witch to kill."

As the guys walk away Nia casts more things at Kevin and he calms down with the trying to shout, which is quickly replaced by panting. Good night, she dumped him right into it. I shake my head as we walk away.

Thirty

JASMINE

When we get out of the library my yard is filled with shifters. I met all these people, but somehow I thought more of them were part of the castle staff, not part of our pack. I wasn't expecting to have so many people here. "Banner, how many adults are in our pack?"

He grins, "You called it our pack." He sweeps me up in a quick hug, when he sets me down he says, "There are roughly 40 fighting adults in our pack."

"Is that a normal pack size?"

"Eh, my personal pack may be a little inflated. Just because of the status thing, more want to be part of this pack. So, even with all the screening I do, we end up with a lot more than would be usual."

"So your parents pack must be huge, right?"

"Well, not exactly. My parents aren't exactly typical. They have ten in their pack, I believe?"

"Oh. Well. I guess that isn't surprising. Ok. I guess we need to figure out how to get everyone there. They are southeast of town, in a house at a crossroads. I think we need to... You know, I just remembered a spell Hekate taught me. She said I shouldn't use it too much but with it, I can get us all there quick. We just need someplace a little more secluded than this. Pretty sure my nosy ass neighbors are watching with all these people on my lawn. Let's wander out into the woods. That will work."

Banner and Leonidas share a look before they start moving through the crowd and telling people to follow me into the woods as I start around the house toward the back. A glance behind tells me that the pack is following and I lead a line of them into the woods behind my house. Banner and Leonidas catch up to me after the whole pack is inside the tree line. We keep moving further in to be away from any prying eyes. Once we get far enough in I string together the spell as she taught it to me, keeping in mind a spot down the road from where the map showed him to be. Luckily, on the other side of this we will just sort of appear, at the most the air will look a little hazy in that spot. The spell cast I tell them, "You all have to go first, when I come through it will close behind me. I am not well versed in the area, so maybe first one through look around and then report back how we are going to go about things?"

Leonidas says, "I'll go. Give me, wait. Does it drain you to hold this?"

"Oh, no. It might if I held it for three hours or something. Hekate mostly doesn't want people remembering how to do this because it could be problematic if too many people start flitting from one place to another like this."

He chuckles, "Ok then. Give me five minutes." He steps

through the portal and is gone. I pace and Banner watches the portal intently while we wait. He is gone for six minutes and we are starting to worry when he steps back through. "We come out very close to the back of the property on a dirt road. The whole area is wooded and really, we only need to go through and step right or left to back into the woods. I went and did a little recon, they are all in the house. Your girl Nia is creative as hell and I have some new ideas. Hake has it playing on the wall in the house. Frank's pack is watching it with him. From what I can tell, they have no idea that we have left, and they aren't patrolling the place either. I couldn't smell anyone until I got up near the house."

Banner announces, "You heard him, everyone through the portal and melt into the woods. If you want to shift, do it after you get into the woods there, so you will have clothes nearby if we leave a different way."

The group is amazingly quiet as they file through. I notice a lot of them are looking at me as they pass so I try to smile and look encouraging as they pass. Banner notices and realizes what is going on, "Stop staring assholes. Get through the portal, plenty of time to see her later." Looking over at me he says, "They are just curious about you. It will pass eventually."

Smiling I tell him, "It's fine. I would be curious too if my prince and pack lead had suddenly gone an married some weird creature that we were now going to fight for. I feel like a little staring is fine at this point."

The last few of the pack slip through the portal, followed by Banner. Leonidas slips my hand onto his arm and say, "M'lady, allow me to escort you."

"Thank sir, your aid is greatly appreciated," I tell him in

my best southern belle voice. We laugh as we walk through the portal.

<hr>

The area they chose to hide in is very rural. I think it likely there isn't a neighbor for miles. Which is great. For us. Thankfully, it is full night as we come through. The portal pops closed behind me and we step back into the trees. Banner appears beside me, "They are still watching the illusion. Nia is good, but I am going to have problems looking her in the eye after this."

"Luckily you don't work with her much, I think you'll have some time before that is a concern. So, how do we want to handle this?"

One of the pack members clears their throat, "I don't think they are watching the show anymore."

We look over and they are all filing outside, Demetris is being dragged by two shifters. There is a gasp as we see how rough all the shifters look. They are emaciated and almost look like they aren't entirely in control... "Oh Gods, he wouldn't. Did he really? What is going to happen to them when I kill him?"

Banner and Leonidas look hard at me, Leonidas says, "What do you mean?"

"I mean, I think, it looks like he has used the control spell on them. On all of them. Look at them, do most packs look like everyone is strung out? I think he has been controlling them but hasn't been allowing for them to care for themselves. And I'm the abomination? Really?"

Banner frowns, "That changes things. We can't kill people forced to actions on someone else's behalf. It looks like there is maybe ten of them, fifteen tops. We have twice their numbers. All we need is a way to contain them."

"Fuck. Fuck. Fuck. I did not study for this. Um... Shit. How can we do this? Keep an eye on the asshole over there and let me try to figure something out," I tell them as I pace. Obviously they know we are here somewhere, even if they aren't sure where. But how can I create something to contain them that doesn't risk one of our people getting stuck in with them? I can create a space to contain them, that is no problem. If I make that sort of space I would still be able to move through it so how can I extend that... Oh. I know! Blood. My blood. If I mark them with my blood that should enable them to move in and out while containing the ones without it. As long as my blood doesn't splash on a bunch of them, it should be fine. "I think I know how, but we have to test it quickly. Who has aspirations to being a guinea pig?"

I see multiple people grin and a few raise their hands even as they shake their heads at how I asked. "Fabulous. Come over here." I throw a quick containment spell on a small area while they walk over. Then, I use my teeth to cut my thumb, it hurts but only for a moment. I swipe a little blood across the back of the hands of two of them, leaving the third as my control. "Ok, you all, walk in to this area," I tell them as I walk around to delineate the space. "All of you try to walk back out the way you came, but if you meet resistance stop. It will be very unpleasant if you try to force your way out."

One of them says, "You said try. Does that mean it could hold us from leaving?"

"Yeah, of course. That's the idea, right? We want to capture Frank's pack, but not hurt them any more than we absolutely have to, so a containment area."

"And if we try to leave by force?"

"That's going to hurt a fucking lot and it won't do you any good either. But, we can answer all the extra questions later, for now, give this a go."

They seem dubious as they walk in, take a couple more steps and turn to walk back out. The two with my blood on them pass through just fine. The one without can't. I reach in after giving my thumb a fresh bite, smear it on them and poof, walks right on out.

"Ok, so now we know this works, line up and I will dab my blood onto your backs under your shirts, where it is less likely to come off. Unfortunately, I don't know a spell to make it stick. So, maybe try not to go in if at all possible, okay? If my blood is on them they will be able to walk out too. Things I never dreamed I would be doing, this probably tops the list, you know?" I have to reopen the wound numerous times to get everyone blooded, but it is done faster than it felt like it was happening. "Have we got a plan for dealing with this? My only plan so far is get to Hake, I figure the kill him part is easy. You all have the more difficult job of rounding up, shit." I turn and expand the containment area so it is big enough to hold the shifters that need to go in it. I line it up with some trees and throw some random colors on the corner trees to help them see where they are aiming. "Sorry, I forgot to make it big enough. Where are we at with this?"

Leonidas and Banner are grinning, and Leonidas says, "We are pretty certain he doesn't know that everyone is here. Banner and myself are the only ones that went near the house, if he has any sort of security system, he probably saw that. Or maybe his shifters smelled us. Who knows. We are thinking the three of us go out like we are alone and—"

"He seems to be putting a cattle prod to the man in chains."

Banner looks that way, "Ok, so, everyone, wait here until I give the signal or we get attacked. Then you get the wolves into the containment as quickly as possible. You know you can run straight through and they will get stopped. If you would like to avoid the fighting with someone you are trying not to injure."

"Hey, what's the signal?"

Banner laughs, "I'll smack her ass or his."

Leonidas laughs, "Well, that will certainly have them focused on us after the things they were watching."

I take a deep breath and start toward where they are jabbing Demetris with a cattle prod. I don't know how it is that he isn't screaming in agony. I sure hope he stays calm after we rescue him or a lot of shifters are going to die. The instant I step out of the tree line Hake smiles at me. I can't wait to kill him. That smile makes me sick and angry. Heading for him I watch his eyes flick to either side of me and narrow, I smile, knowing he sees Leonidas and Banner. Hake sends most of his wolves toward us and I hear a loud smack! Before me the wolves stop as a group, jaws dropping all over. Hake recovers first and says, "Go get them!"

About that time I hear the sound of many feet pounding the ground toward us and his wolves look nervous. I run toward Hake, leaping at him, and falling right through the illusion that I jumped at. Son of a bitch! Standing I grab the wolf poking Demetris with the cattle prod and toss him toward the others. The wolves under Hake's control are fighting like berserkers. I lean over Demetris, "If I let you go, will you try not to kill the wolves from Frank's pack?"

He nods and whispers painfully, "I know they are under

his control. You'll find him in the woods over there." He points to an area above his head, by angling his head in that direction. "He's waiting for you. Be careful." I nod and use magic to set him free. I step back as he rolls off the table and is shifted before he hits the ground. He roars and the shifters freeze briefly, giving some of our pack the opportunity to grab them and haul them off to the containment area. I head for the woods again, on my way to Hake and a meeting with his destiny.The tree line is thin and there is a small hill. Hake is at the crest of it and of course, he has some wolves with him. Happily only three. He sends them running at me, I hit the first one with a really nasty spell that leaves him on the ground twitching. The next one is nearly at me, I bend my knees a little and hit him with an up swing to the base of his diaphragm. While he is gasping for air the other one leaps at me and I drop to the side, rolling and coming back up I hit him with the same nasty spell I hit his friend with. Shielding myself, can't believe I forgot that, I hit the one still trying to get his diaphragm to work properly with that nasty spell. When they all finally quit twitching they are never going to want to see me again. That taken care of I turn to Hake. He starts firing shots at me and I let some pass me by, the ones that would be a pain to dodge I sling back at him. I am not really aiming with those but I manage to singe him a few times. He on the other hand, mostly shoots like a those white suited guys in the movies that never hit anything on purpose.

I finally make it up the hill to him and he is firing shots at me hard now, I don't bother with moving, my shield absorbs the hits. Reaching out I grab an arm and the back of his neck, then something hits me hard and I go flying.

Hekate

I can do nothing but watch as Cronos blasts my Jasmine away from Hake. Once he does that, I appear directly in front of him, my sword in hand. His eyes widen but I am already swinging for his neck. My sword is sharp and his head flies away with ease. Finally, after all this time. Vengeance.

I pull the spell Jasmine set on those wolves off of them and set them on Hake, still laying unconscious where Jasmine dropped him when Cronos blasted her. Anger surges in me at his interference and I give his body a solid kick. That isn't quite enough so I use my sword to stab him a few more times before I call Hades to take the fool to Tartarus. He knew the penalty for interference. Leonidas and Banner run through the trees and make a bee line for Jasmine. They are so good for her. I watch as they tend her together, ensuring she is alive and waiting impatiently for her to revive. Their faces are the first things she sees as her eyes flutter open. She starts to cry when she wakes, thinking Hake is still alive somewhere. They reassure her that their are wolves from Frank's pack eating him right now. She says, "Oh thank the Goddess!" and then cries harder. Her mates hold her gently as she cries, though they both look puzzled.

I can't wait to see their faces when they figure it out.

Thirty-One

JASMINE

It has been a few weeks since Hake died. The wolves of Frank's pack came by and apologized as they were on their way out of town. They said they just didn't want to stick around a place with so many bad memories and I couldn't talk them out of it. Now, I am sitting in my back yard on the sun, watching the crew work on our house. I bought the two places next to mine, they were willing to sell once I told them I would pay for the land and for their houses to be moved to a new plot of land. The ones that shot at me while I was in wolf form jumped on the deal fast. It made me wonder if they suspected something but since they were moving away now, I decided not to concern myself with it.

Once those houses were gone, the guys jumped right into expanding and remodeling the house. The only room currently untouched is my bedroom. Once the new one is built I'll move in there and they'll finish that space too. The delivery people in this area love us now and know us by name. I hope we will have it done sometime in the next month or two, the delivery is great but getting old.

Speaking of, here is pizza now. I hope up and walk over to the car, digging some cash out of my pocket to go along with the electronic tip I sent, The kid stacks the pizzas up in my arms, well used to our shenanigans now. They leave and I take the pizzas to the porch calling out to everyone that the pizza is here and it is break time. Setting the stack on the table we have out here, I grab a slice from the top box and take a bite as Banner and Leonidas get to the porch. I wait for Banner to get a slice and I hand Leonidas a glass of blood I called from the fridge.

"So, guys. I have noticed a strange thing happening. I am hoping you might be able to shed some light on..." They both freeze and their eyes meet. I know they set this in motion, but why? "I have noticed that the people that live in this area seem to be moving at an unparalleled rate. Just up and running out of the area. Any idea why?"

Leonidas sips from his glass., "I told you she would notice."

Banner glares at him, "We might have encouraged the pack and his family," he jerks a thumb toward Leonidas, "to move to the area."

I think about this as I chew the bite in my mouth, "Why?"

Leonidas takes this one saying, "Safety in numbers. It is easier for us all to stay safe if we are surrounded by our people. But we weren't sure how you would feel about that. So, Banner here said, well, she can't do anything about it if we suggest it and finance it for those that need help. I told him you would notice, but it would be fun to see how long it took. Speaking of which, Banner, pay up."

"You bet on it? What were the terms?"

Now they both blush and I cross my arms over my chest as I wait for the explanation. Banner shrugs and says, "Well, I bet two hundred that I could keep you occupied enough that you wouldn't notice till the street was refilled and Leonidas said you would notice before everyone was out. We also may have thrown some sexual favors in the pot..."

"Like?"

Leonidas grins, "You'll see tonight, since I won. Don't worry, you'll be appreciative of the bet a lot more then."

Did you love this book? Please leave a review, it really helps. Thank you for journeying with my friends!

Also by Rhiannon Futch

The Daughter of the Moon series-

<u>Selena Rose, Daughter of the Moon Book 1</u>

<u>Thorns of the Rose, Daughter of the Moon Book 2</u>

<u>Heart of the Rose, Daughter of the Moon Book 3</u>

The Fate's Chronicles series

<u>A Vampire's Fate</u>

<u>A Vampire's Treasure</u>

<u>A Vampire's Dream</u>

<u>A Vampire's Chase</u>

<u>A Vampire's Fight</u>

<u>Fated for Halloween -</u> only available via email signup

The Belancore Witches of North Carolina series

<u>Witchy Ever After</u>

<u>A Witchy New Year</u>

<u>My Witchy Valentine</u>

Sin series

<u>Sin on a Dark Knight</u>

<u>Sin on a Broken Heart</u>

<u>Sin on a Burning Heart</u>

Sin on a Vengeful Heart

The Vampire Kings Series

Mercy of the Vampire King

Shame of the Vampire King

Pursuit of the Vampire King

Prey of the Vampire King

Reign of the Vampire King

Coming Soon

Love and Vampires Series

Olivia's Fall

Olivia's Prison

Olivia's Flight

Olivia's Family

Warriors of the Old Gods

A Dream of Blood

A Dream of Wolves

A Dream of Stone

A Dream of Ravens

A Dream of Bones